Trails

R.A. Abell

Rovell Enterprises Ltd.
Kanata, Ontario, Canada.

Front Cover Photo: © Dr. Bob Abell

ISBN-10: 1494900572
ISBN-13: 978-1494900571

DEDICATION

To my wife, my children Kendrick and Deanna, and to the seven generations that come after.

ACKNOWLEDGMENTS

Editing: Evelyn A Abell, Christine Feldman

Thanks to Dr. Francois Mai for his review of the medical treatment section in Chapter 22.

CONTENTS

Chapter 1 — Up the Trail

The day was warm for April, even by Arizona standards. Shelley found herself pausing more frequently than usual as she climbed higher in the canyon. Though it was still early, the sun was already intense. Stopping, she perched on one of the large boulders that frequently littered the trail, surveying the site with a practiced eye.

A small urosaurus ornatus, sunning himself on a nearby snag, turned to assess the threat, then returned to his sentinel pose, soaking up the morning rays. Shelley smiled to herself as she watched. Her fascination with lizards and snakes had been intense ever since her early teens, when her father had first set up his business in the area.

Her science projects for the next three years had regularly featured various species of small lizards — carefully caught, fed, displayed, and returned to their original location. In fact, it was her fascination with these creatures — and their ability to survive the often-harsh desert conditions — that put her on her career path as an ecologist.

She wondered sometimes if she was overdoing it. Her undergrad years had been a blast. Learning came easily, she was social and athletic, and she breezed through without much stress — and without serious attachments.

Her father's solar installations in the desert had required environmental assessments, and three years of fieldwork assisting seasoned professionals in their research and reporting had passed quickly. She was not quite sure what possessed her to decide to pursue a Ph.D.

Still, Michael was amazing to work with. As her adviser, he pushed her hard. With his depth of experience and knowledge of desert fauna, he opened her eyes to a much larger picture, and threw into sharp focus how humankind was ignoring the basic rules of the survival game.

A slight movement in a patch of sagebrush to her right jolted her out of retrospection. Snake! Most likely a rattler hunting for breakfast. Probably best to move on. Shelley had often encountered rattlers in her years of hiking these hills, and knew they were not a problem as long as they did not feel threatened. Most bites resulted from stupidity.

She smiled at the memory of the classic description given by a park ranger. *"Most rattlesnake bites involve high levels of testosterone mixed with alcohol."* She had met more than a few of that type working on some of her Dad's projects. On occasion, she had to verbally bite one of them herself!

Slipping the water bottle into the pocket of her pack, she collected her walking stick, adjusted the Nikon D610 around her neck, and continued up the path.

An hour later, she crested an intermediate ridge and surveyed the canyon stretching upward in the distance. The only sounds were the sharp trills and squeals of a pair of nearby Canyon Towhees, and the harsh chatter of Cactus Wrens.

The Canyon Towhee population had been in decline for more than two decades, and although very widespread and not of concern for extinction, Shelley wondered what had changed in the ecology of the region to account for the decline. Interesting — if not very tractable as a potential thesis topic! She had heard the lecture from her Dad on several occasions: *"Don't strive for the 'great work'. Pick something appropriate for study — and get it done."*

But she was still fascinated by these interesting birds — particularly in the protective nature of the male, and how it played into the environment of the area.

As she tried to focus on the Towhee calls, she was annoyed by the sudden echo of a large jet as it crossed above the canyon. The narrow canyon's curved sides seemed to amplify the sound. She could see large contrails streaming out behind. Strange. The jet didn't seem to be that high. Usually one would not see that much of a trail unless it was a very long way up.

As she followed the jet with her eyes, turning toward the left side of the path, she saw an ocotillo in full bloom. A tiny hummingbird was visiting the colorful flowers high up on each stem. Whipping her camera into position, she took a burst of pictures, catching the jet, the contrail, and the tiny hummingbird in the same shot. Thumbing in new settings each time, she took two more burst shots before the tiny bird darted to the other side of the plant. *"Hope some of those are useable,"* she thought.

The rumble from the jet faded as quickly as it had appeared, and Shelley focused again on locating the towhees. Rounding an outcrop, camera at the ready, she found the typical towhee domestic scene. The male ruffled his feathers, and trilled brightly, keeping protective watch over his mate, who was feeding beneath the small ironwood tree. As the female moved, he followed closely above, always on the alert for predators. Shelley carefully checked a nearby boulder for biting or stinging things, then settled with her camera and notebook.

"Considering the places I wander, I could do with having my own private sentry watching my back," she thought with a wry smile. She'd had a few potentials, but tended to be pretty fussy with the company she kept, as well as a spot feisty, and no one had quite measured up to the task to date.

Another hour passed, and Shelley became aware that something unusual was happening. Though it was just after noon, there seemed a moderately heavy haze developing overhead, and she had to twice reset her camera to get enough light. She had actually checked the forecast before setting out, knowing that it was dangerous to be wandering though narrow canyons when rain was expected. There was nothing to even suggest rain in the forecast.

Then she realized that the haze actually followed the path where the jet had passed earlier, and to the west and north there were similar patterns in the sky. Instinctively she reached for her camera and captured this strange pattern. Further to the north some substantial cloud was building, looking like thunderclouds. Hastily packing her notebook and the remains of her lunch, she started back down the canyon.

By the time Shelley crossed the intermediate ridge, the sky was looking nasty, and although it was only a bit after two, it was surprisingly dark. *"Damn,"* she thought, *"I didn't plan for crap weather. With only this light Nylon shell, it could be dangerous to be stuck up here."*

She felt the first cold drops of rain. Looking at her camera, she realized she had not put the lens cap back. As she searched her pockets, a wave of heavy mist swept over and past her. She closed her eyes and wrinkled her nose. The air had a sudden acrid sulfurous smell. As she snapped the lens cap in place, she noticed that both her camera and her jacket seemed to have a fine whitish coating.

Then the rain started in earnest. Quickly zipping the camera inside her jacket, she continued down the trail. *"At least the rain is cleaning up that foul smell,"* she thought. *"I've never run into that before. Sort of a cross between downtown L.A. on a bad day and a garbage dump! Whatever would cause that out here in the desert? The air is always so fresh."*

She entered another narrow canyon, the bottom littered with the coarse boulders and gravel typical of a wash. The rain had temporarily slowed, but she stopped abruptly and looked ahead.

"Don't even think about it! It could flood in a heartbeat! Come up here!"

She was sure her own heart missed a couple of beats, before starting to pound. Shelley looked up the slope to where a small ledge was apparent — perhaps twenty feet up.

"Don't stand there gawking! Get your butt in gear."

R.A. Abell

Chapter 2 — Knave or Knight?

She looked again at the wash, then turned and started up the slope. The footing was treacherous and she had to thread her way carefully. It became steeper as she climbed.

"Here, catch this." A coil of fine climbing rope snaked past her head. "Loop it around that pretty waist, and get with the program."

Filing the offhand compliment, she did as he suggested. At that moment there was rapid swooshing sound below her, quickly turning to a roar, as the flood flashed through the canyon floor. She clung to the rope, hugged the rock, and closed her eyes.

"You're fine. Missed you by a good three feet, now keep on climbing".

"Bossy bugger," she thought with a little smile. Why did the image of the male towhee flit through her mind?

He extended a hand and helped her onto the ledge. She had another shock when she followed the rope to where it circled a small boulder — something, but not enough to have held her weight — especially if she had ended up in the water. He had tied his fate to hers, by looping it around his own waist before throwing it to her!

Still holding her outstretched hand, he smiled from under the hood of his rain suit. "I'm Pete".

"Shelley".

"OK. So now that the formal stuff is done, let's get out of this weather."

The ledge was wider than it appeared from below. At the back she could see that Pete had draped a tarp over a small cave, holding the corners down crudely with rocks. She got down and slid gratefully behind the tarp, followed closely by her companion.

"Sorry I didn't have time to spiffy things up. I hadn't expected company, though I had spotted you earlier when you crossed the ridge. I was a bit concerned for you. Rather unusual to see a girl out here by herself." As he talked, he wiggled out of his rain suit, folded it, and stacked it in the corner.

It was roomier than was apparent from the outside, but still quite cramped for two. *"Good thing Pete is not a lot bigger than I am,"* Shelley thought.

"I've spent many years wandering these mountains, and am used to taking care of myself. In all kinds of situations," she added pointedly.

Pete grinned inwardly at the barb, but kept a serious face. "I'm sure you are," he replied. "Nonetheless, I'm glad I was here."

She studied his face for a moment, noting the slim face with a strong chin, and the teasing sparkle in his eyes that showed even in the gloom of the cave. "Guess I have to admit that under these circumstances, so am I ," she replied, still hearing the roar of the water as it continued down though the canyon below.

"Right. Now we need to get you out of those wet clothes. Do you have any dry things in your pack?

Shelley tried to push back the sudden panic from her voice. "The only dry things I have are the bottom zip-off legs of my cargo pants."

Pete broke out in laughter. "Now that conjures up quite an image, but we don't have a trench coat for you."

Shelley tried to suppress them, but the short burst of giggles was having none of it, and had to erupt as a series of snorts! She quickly got them under control, but was afraid the damage was already done.

Still chuckling, Pete rolled away from her and rifled through his pack, presenting her with a pair of stretchy cotton boxers, a white tee, dry socks, a thin pullover, and dungarees.

The panic returned. "I'll be okay."

"Look, you seem like a really bright girl, even if you do look like B-grade movie star. You know about hypothermia. From what I'm hearing outside, we are here at least until tomorrow morning. In another half hour it will be too dark to safely get down, even if there were no chance of further flash floods or slides. Are we agreed on this latter point?"

"It's not looking too good out there," she admitted — then added with a grin and mock indignation, "but what do you mean 'B-grade'!"

"Well, you're only maybe twenty-two, twenty-three. It's not about the looks; it's about the experience. If you were A-grade, you would already be used to taking it all off in front of a camera, never mind a poor engineering student who promises to keep his back turned — as difficult as that will be!"

Her laughter suppression systems failed her for a second time. "I'm twenty-five actually, but you're right, I'm still camera shy," she laughed. "How about I change inside your sleeping-bag?"

"No dice! We need that to stay dry! Do you have any idea how cold it could get tonight? I'm a man of my word, and I have now turned my back, so get with the program. And here, this has touched my bod, but it's the best I can offer," he said, passing her a small towel over his shoulder."

"We need that dry," she thought. Yes, that would be the next challenge. Not that she had never shared a bed with a man. But for her, casual sex had proved far from ideal, and she just wasn't going there again. She wanted the whole package. And a single sleeping bag would be tight quarters in which to keep one's distance. Well, that was the reality.

She removed her soaked jacket, pulled one of the dry cargo-pant legs from her pack, and carefully dried the exterior of her camera. She noted that so much water had made it through the jacket, that all traces of residue from the strange mist was gone.

She unbuttoned and removed her shirt, checked that Pete was still firmly faced to the wall, and slipped off her bra. It could not have been wetter if she had gone swimming in it.

She toweled her cold skin. It certainly did feel better to be out of those wet duds.

"If you need any help, just ask," Pete volunteered, still facing his side of the cave.

"You're very accommodating, but I am managing just fine thank you," she snapped back, while pulling the dry tee over her head, followed by the sweater. Not that easy a task lying on one's back with a very low roof overhead, and another body just inches away on the side.

"Okay, your call entirely."

"It certainly does feel better to have a dry shirt on, she commented. I guess I should thank you for insisting on this."

"You're welcome. My shirt never had it so good."

The boots and pants proved somewhat more difficult. First, there was no way she could get to her laces. "Uh-oh. Houston, we have a problem. Guess I do need some help — with my boots."

"Damsel in distress? At your service. ... Hey careful! Those things are wet and muddy. Can you hike yourself in a bit further?"

"I think so, hang on."

"Damn good thing I'm not claustrophobic," she thought as she wormed her upper body another two feet into the narrow space at the back of the small cave.

"Okay. That's good."

She felt the laces come free, and his hand carefully supporting her ankle while each boot was wiggled free. She briefly realized how vulnerable she was in this position, her upper body essentially immobilized by the low ceiling.

"These are so wet, I am going to stick them outside to wash the dirt off, if that's okay with you. We can dry them later."

"Knock yourself out," she replied. There was only a tiny change in the light as he moved the tarp aside, and then returned to his place.

"Where did you put that towel?" he asked while he stripped off her socks. She found it and passed it down to where his waiting hand grazed her knee.

She felt him toweling her frozen feet vigorously.

"These feet are like friggen icebergs. I might have to reconsider letting you in that sleeping bag tonight! OK, best I can do. Anything else?"

"Don't sound so hopeful."

"Hey, it's not every day a knight comes across a beautiful damsel in distress. Have to make the best of it.

"I think the rain might be lightening up a little," he continued. "If we are really lucky, we might have a chance for a spot of a fire before we have to turn in. That would give some chance for you to warm those cold feet before I let them in my sleeping bag."

"That would be good, but for now, back to your sentinel post Lancelot, while I finish this job."

"Yes M'Lady". He handed her back the towel and she heard him roll back to his left to face the wall.

She wormed her way back out of the narrow confines, and got her hips up enough to get her shorts and panties off and the towel under her bottom. But actually getting them over her feet without rolling on her side was a non-starter. She finally managed it, but not without bumping her bare butt solidly against her cave-mate.

"Hmmm. Nice firm bottom. Good muscle tone. M'Lady must ride to hounds on a regular basis."

"Cut the wisecracks, Lancelot, and just keep your attention on the wall. You won't have to put up with my butt for much longer."

"No hurry. No hurry at all. Take all the time you need."

That turned out to be longer than she expected. The stretch cotton boxers were not bad, and they fit her upper thigh snugly. The dungarees were a whole different story. Getting them over her feet was one thing, but when she got to the hips, it was clearly no go.

"Seems our hips and butts are built a spot differently."

"Well, I think that's a good thing!"

"Maybe, but these dungarees don't cut it. Any other ideas?"

She rolled onto her back again, and draped the jeans over his now barely visible form. She squinted her eyes as the cave was suddenly illuminated by a LED camp lantern. Pete rummaged though his pack, then rolled onto his right elbow and smiled at her.

"You're decent, and I have to say those clothes have never looked so good. Nice legs. You're dry now, so why don't you slip into the sleeping bag and warm up some more. You have been pretty lucid — almost too much so at times," he teased, " — so I don't think you are in further danger from hypothermia. It sounds like the rain has stopped, so maybe I should go out and get some wood and see if we can complete the warm up process."

"I should come outside and call my Dad. If I don't arrive back by seven or so, he'll have the army out. And don't say anything when I talk to him. If he hears a male voice on the line under these conditions, he and a bunch of his construction workers will be on their way up with baseball bats."

"If you're going out there, take those socks off. I don't have any more dry ones. … Spot protective, isn't he? You did say you're twenty-five."

"I'll still be 'Daddy's little girl' when I'm forty. He wouldn't be concerned if he knew where I was and whom I was with in normal circumstances. Trapped in a canyon by a storm doesn't quite qualify as normal. Nor does sharing a sleeping bag with a shady character with questionable motives," she grinned, as she slipped outside. "So just hush up!"

"Wait a second. Before you stand out in the cold, I have an idea." He went back inside and returned with a piece of soft leather about four-feet square. "I use this for laying out my samples. It's pretty clean right now, and it will break the wind."

Taking a short length of rope, he folded one edge over the rope, circled the leather around her waist, and tied it snugly at one side. The temperature difference was immediate.

She smiled brightly at him, took her cell phone out, and brought one finger to her lip in the "shush" sign. She knew that this canyon was angled toward the main road, and that the cell tower was just on the opposite side. It would be close to maximum range, but she had called from this area before. He answered on the first ring.

"Yes, it's me. ... Yes, I'm just fine. ... I'm sure you were worried. I would have called earlier but was hunkered down out of the storm. .... Yes, but I'm going to have to stay overnight. I was still pretty high up when the storm struck, and I couldn't cross the wash. ... No, I found a small cave. No, it does not have any 'wild' occupants." She grinned at Pete.

"Listen Dad, I'm warm, I'm dry, I have food and water. Remember this isn't the first time I've been overnight up here. ... I'll be fine! But my cell is not fully charged, and I want to give you a call in the morning before I head down, so I need to sign off now while I have lots of battery power left.

"Love you. ... Yes, yes, I know. Relax, have a glass of wine for me. ..."

"I'll call you first thing in the morning. Yes, before eight.
Sleep well; I've got to go. ...Yes, bye."

"You could have used my phone if yours was low".

"No problem. I charged mine overnight. It's not 'fully
charged' like I said, but it's actually fine. If we talked more,
he would worry more. And maybe want me to call back
three times through the night. I need to conserve more
than the battery."

"You must have given him lots of reason to worry over the
years."

"Yes, I probably did, but then he brought me up to be the
person I am. Mom left us to take a job overseas when I was
about twelve. Her career was more important to her than
the family.

It was hard to take for a while, for Dad especially, but our
life settled into a rhythm after we moved here. I had always
been closer to him, so didn't miss her as much as I might
have. Probably made me a bit of a tomboy."

"A B-grade, movie-star-tomboy — with an attitude. Quite a
handful for anyone."

Rotating her by the hips, he steered her back to the cave.
"Okay, cell call's done. Get those cold tootsies into that
sleeping bag. I'll let you know when the fire is ready. I'm
going to snag some of the dead-fall brought down by that
flood."

Stooping to enter the cave, Shelley looked back over her shoulder. "Please be careful down there. It could be very slippery."

As she ducked under the tarp, she found herself surprised by the depth of emotion that had attended that warning. This was Miss No-attachments, Leave-Them-Laughing-When-You-Go Shelley girl. What's going on here?

The bladder signal was sudden. She removed the leather "skirt" and headed back outside. Pete had already disappeared over the edge. At least on this occasion he had taken the time to secure the rope to an appropriately sized boulder. She moved to the far end of the ledge, dropped her boxers, and lowered the level in the reservoir. Then she hustled back to the cave, stretched out Pete's sleeping bag, and quickly snuggled inside — her head still buzzing with the events of the day.

R.A. Abell

Chapter 3 — Light of the Fire

She must have dropped off, because it seemed only moments later that she heard branches snapping, and shortly after saw the flickering yellow light of the fire. She was torn between the snug comfort of the sleeping bag and the attraction of the fire — as well as the fire-keeper. While she was still wrestling with this, Pete poked his head under the tarp.

"Any interest in some grilled trout"?

"What? Where did you get a trout?"

"Poor bugger was flopping around in a tiny pool off to the side of the wash. Must have been flooded out of a lake further up. The rough ride down wasn't very kind to him. I thanked him for offering himself, and ended his misery. Looks pretty good on the spit though. You hungry?"
Her body answered the summons. Almost 8 hours had passed since she last ate.

"You might want the skirt. Shame to hide those legs, but the air is chilly. Can I give you a hand with it?"

She stood patiently while he adjusted the leather and re-tied the cord. Then he ducked back inside, and brought out the sleeping bag.

"This is Shelley-pre-warmed, so we might just as well take advantage of it as well."

They sat side by side on a piece of dead-fall straddling two small rocks. Pete brought the opened sleeping bag around their shoulders. Between the sleeping bag, the fire, and some shared body heat, Shelley was quite comfortable in the crisp air. The sky had cleared, and the stars filled the sky from horizon to horizon.

The trout was a good size, but it didn't take them long to reduce it to skin and bone. This Pete threw back to the bottom of the wash, to avoid attracting any animals to their shelf.

They sat quietly for a while, just enjoying the stars, the fire, and the patient company. After some time, Shelley broke the silence.

"You're pretty resourceful. I haven't ever had that good a meal in a restaurant."

"Mademoiselle flatters the chef. Nothing but ze best should ever pass zhese pretty lips."

She looked at him with amusement. "Do you ever stop with the flattery?"

"No," he said seriously, "Not when it is sincere."

"You never told me why you were up here, and what did you mean when you said this leather was used to hold your samples?"

"I was looking for rocks. I trained as a geologist, and still have the fascination. Too bad there are no jobs, unless I want to work for a shale-oil company. I might be shady, but not that shady. So I enrolled in advanced placement in engineering. For the summer, best I could find was work over at Chemulous."

"What do they do?"

"I'm not really sure. I've only been there for a month. Must be important though. I had to sign a non-disclosure and employment contract that was the size of a community phone book. All I know is that we get daily shipments of concentrated chemicals from a sister plant somewhere south of the border, and I have to draw a sample from each vat, run it through a spectrum analyzer, and put the results in the computer."

"So what's in the stuff?"

He smiled at the thought a girl was even interested in what he did. Most of the girls he knew would have said *'who cares'*, or at best, *'through a what...?'*

"According to that document I signed, I could do twenty years if I told you."

Hugging her shoulder on the excuse of adjusting the sleeping bag they were using as a blanket, he added, "There are better ways I can think of to spend the next twenty years."

Her pulse raced, and she flushed a little at the seemingly offhand movement and attached comment. "Slow down Shelley girl. Not a good time to lose your cool. You're not prepared for that, and I doubt he is either. This wasn't a planned date. Yes. I know. There are no 'coincidences', but let's take time to make sure of the message."

Pete stirred the dying fire with his stick. Then putting it down, took her hand, caressed it briefly with his thumb, and pressed it to his lips. "Sleep time M'Lady. Wood's gone, it's getting desert-cold already, and you told your poor suffering father that you would call before eight."

Getting up and wrapping the bag around her, he added, "But before we turn in, head over there and do your business. Once we're zipped in, I don't want you needing out in the middle of the night. I'll use the other end of the ledge. And don't you dare pee on that bag!"

Shelley snorted. "Yes. Sir ... Lancelot. I'll be careful. You just attend to you're own business."

By the time Shelley returned to the cave, Pete was already down to boxers and tee shirt, and organizing the sleeping space. Shelley stretched the bag out in the narrow confines, climbed on and flipped the top over her body. Grinning, she said, "OK, you can zip me in. Where are you going to sleep?"

"You know very well M'Lady," Pete replied with an answering grin, zipping the bottom and settling in on the side she had conveniently left for him. "I see I get to guard the door with the cold zipper."

"Isn't that what knights do?" she asked innocently.

"I have to get the bloody thing done up first. Scrunch over a bit more. There! This wasn't designed for two, but we'll manage. Kinda cozy actually."

He leaned over suddenly and gave her a peck on the cheek. "Sleep tight. A bit cool now, but if you get too warm, you do have a layer to shed."

"In your dreams, Lancelot".

"Yes, quite likely."

She laughed, and rolled on her side. He felt pressure from her back.

"Darn!"

"Problem," he asked?"

"I always sleep on my side — fetal position. It's not working in this space."

"Okay. I can work with that. We just have to move at the same time. Try now."

Shelley rolled to her left, and felt Pete cuddle in behind her, his left arm lazily draped round her waist.

"Is that better?" he asked.

Shelley didn't fully trust her response, so went with a fairly non-committal, "It works".

A moment later, she felt a slight pressure on her lower back. "Go to sleep!" Pete said.

"I was planning on that. I don't need you telling me."

"I wasn't talking to you."

Shelley snorted.

"Well, I guess that answers the question of whether you're gay," she laughed. "How are you going to explain this to your girlfriend."

"My ex-girlfriend, you mean? Couldn't do it. She was a 'nice' small-town girl. We grew up together. Nice like I said, but she found the plot lines and gags in 'Big Bang Theory' were way too difficult. Sort of a female version of 'Zack', if you know the show.

"She preferred contest shows, like that one where you have to guess the price of consumer products. That, and spending time in bed. The idea that a girl would be choosy about who she slept with would simply not compute. Or be interested in anything beyond physical relationships or the latest news in the fashion mags. You could have a more intelligent conversation with a parrot.

"Being a typical male, I have to admit there were some attractive elements to the arrangement, and I think I also was afraid to hurt her feelings — until she attached herself to another stud. I celebrated the 'escape' for a whole week. I'm super happy to say I have stayed on the wagon until now."

"You're still on the wagon Lancelot, and don't forget it."

"Ah, but now I have the incentive to fall off. Will I have to fight any dragons?"

"Just my Dad," she replied, "and the 'dragon lady' if you get out of line. Now go to sleep."

"Hmmm. ... One last question. For the most part you smell pretty good, but your hair in the back has a certain 'Je ne sais quoi' that is slightly reminiscent of my workplace. You been around chemicals lately?"

"Oh, sorry. Probably from that strange mist that hit just before the rain started in earnest. The mist that smelled more or less like a garbage dump?"

"Didn't get that where I was."

"I was still pretty far up the slope. It wasn't very pleasant. Burned my eyes. But I thought most of it washed off when I got soaked."

"Stuff like that sticks to hair. A smelly mist? Interesting. Probably not enough left to analyze — unless we shear you bald."

"No way Sherlock! You're not talking scissors to my hair, even if it is in the name of science."

"Well we have lots of water between us. I can help you wash it in the morning."

"Lancelot, Sherlock, and Jeeves. You're a man of many talents."

"Uh huh," he yawned. "Goodnight Mistress Shelley."

She found sleep did not come easily. Every part of mind and body seemed in turmoil. But finally the systems sorted themselves out, and she dropped into a dreamless sleep.
...

When she finally awoke, daylight was creeping round the edge of the tarp. She tried to stretch, but her arm ran into the low rock roof. The events of the previous day came flooding back. She was slightly chilly, so rolled on her back and reached for Pete. But he was gone. She pulled the tarp back to gaze out.

The sun was emerging over the opposite ridge. She found herself staring at the bottom of Pete's feet, as he was lying prone, watching something in the bottom of the canyon. Before she had time to make a smart remark, Pete put his finger to his lips, and motioned for her to come take a look.

She grabbed her camera and slithered up beside him. Below in the small pool left by the flood, a coyote was splashing about, apparently trying to catch small minnows. He was arching his back and pouncing with both front feet straight out in front of him, making a great splash with each attempt, but obviously having limited success. Shelley quickly popped the lens cap off, and raised the camera to her eye.

Pete heard a small expletive. He looked at her quizzically. She turned the lens toward him and pointed. The UV filter was completely covered in a layer of opaque whitish powder. Shelley unscrewed the filter, handed it to Pete with a whispered "Hold this," and returned to her task. She managed to get her focus and settings just as the coyote made another quick series of little jumps.

This time he obviously must have hit his target, as he held his position for several seconds before flipping a small fish out of the pool and swallowing it in one bite. He washed it down with some of the fresh water, shook himself vigorously — spraying water in every direction — then sauntered happily up the canyon and out of sight around an outcrop of rock.

"Did you get some good shots," Pete asked?

"Yes, I think so. Good thing I had that removable UV filter attached. I could never have cleaned the lens in time. The filter is really there to protect my expensive telephoto. It also cuts out some haze, but in normal light conditions I can manage without it."

"Do you have a case for this?" Pete asked, rotating the filter, studying it, and holding it up to the light."

"Yes, I have it in my pack, but I could just clean it up and put it back."

"Maybe, but then I might have to cut your hair, and I thought you were not keen on that."

"Oh, I get it. You can get a sample to analyze from the filter."

"Bingo. I am of course assuming that this deposit did come from your mystery mist?"

"Yes. I popped the lens cap on before zipping the camera inside my jacket. So when I — and the camera — got soaked, the waterproof cap protected the coating!"

"Okay! Find me that filter case, and then you better get on the blower to your Dad. It is almost eight."

"Yes Sir — Lancelot," she replied with a mock salute.

"And you might want to put the sweater on. That tee shirt is pretty thin. Not that I'm complaining!"

She looked down, and flushed a bit, crossing her arms over her ample chest. "This is almost transparent! Did you deliberately haul out the thinnest you had?"

"Poor student fare," he replied with a grin. "But you really do look spectacular in it."

She put on a sour face, harrumphed in reply, and turned towards the cave. He could see her shoulders shake in a Shelley giggle.

When she returned, the sweater was in place, and she held the filter case in one hand with the leather 'skirt' in the other. "To your duties, Jeeves!"

"Yes, Mistress Shelley," he replied with a low bow.

He slipped the filter in its case and popped it into his pocket. Taking the leather and the cord, he moved close behind her.

"Mistress Shelley has some strange growth on her pretty butt," he said in mock seriousness.

She reached back and slipped her cell phone out of her shorts. "Never you mind my petty butt, Jeeves. Get about your duties, before I freeze."

"Rhyming meter. My lady is a poet as well as beautiful," he commented, tying the cord, folding and smoothing the top of the leather to her hips, and then wrapping his arms round her waist from behind.

"Oh shush," she laughed. "I have to make this call."

She turned her head to smile at him. "That is much warmer. Thank you — for everything. You really have been a perfect gentleman, Lancelot, as well as a handy guy to have around," she said as she dialed the number, "but no misbehaving or heavy breathing while I'm on the phone.

"Hi Dad. Hope you slept well. Yes, I managed just fine. I should make it back to my car about eleven. I could meet you for coffee about eleven-thirty. Oh good night!" She burst into laughter.

"Yes, I'm fine. Something just struck me funny. Got to go. See you at eleven-thirty."

"Did you deliberately stick that where I would see it while I was on the phone?" she laughed, barely able to contain herself. Above and to the right of the cave, her wet clothes were spread out to dry in the sun — bra and panties to the left, shirt and shorts to the right. The bra obviously had two rocks of appropriate size fitted in place. Fireplace charcoal had been used to create an image of a man and woman standing side by side, hand in hand."

"No. That was where the sun hits earliest. You do want your duds dry, I assume. ... The aboriginal rock art was an afterthought."

She rotated to face him, his arms still round her waist.

"Thank you for being on this earth, and for letting me find you. Now let's get moving. I told Dad I would meet him at eleven-thirty, and I have some serious planning to do, figuring out how to explain what happened here — before you meet him! So enough of this cuddly stuff, nice though it is. Have you made my breakfast?"

Chapter 4 — Roy

Roy paced nervously between his truck and Shelley's bright red Fiesta. Twice in the last hour he started up the wash and then thought better of it. It would be too easy to miss, with the multiple small hummocks and low bush that characterized the lower trail. Better to stay here. He walked over to the rather beat up small pickup parked at the wilderness trail head. Arizona plates. He had considered asking the sheriff to run a check, but Bill was pretty busy down the road.

That flood must have been a doozer. The traffic was backed up for at least two miles in both directions while the road crew worked feverishly to get the debris moved and the washouts filled in.

He scanned the lower ridge for the hundredth time. He stopped abruptly mid scan. There was someone coming into view, but it didn't look, or act, like his Shelley Girl. He could recognize her gait at a mile. Sort of a mix of purposeful stride with the occasional skip, bounce, or abrupt halt as something caught her attention.

He remembered with a smile their earliest outings. She had that special joy in creation, which animated her every movement. That joy, and the movement that celebrated it, had stayed with her for over twenty years.

The figure on the ridge stopped, turned, and looked back. A man, with a good-sized backpack. He gestured at something, struck a pose as if he were being photographed, and then turned and continued down.

Suddenly another figure bounced into sight, ran up behind the man, and gave him a playful shove. The man backed off, extended his walking stick like a sword, swiped it a couple of times, then threw his arms in the air.

Shelley, for Roy was certain of that in an instant — even at that great distance — bounced over to merge the two figures briefly into one, before skipping ahead down the path.

"You have some explaining to do, young lady," Roy thought, dabbing at the corner of his eye. He had somehow had the feeling she was okay, and was very relieved that his gut had sent accurate signals. She had been his lifeline ever since Jane left twelve years ago.

But she was a young woman, and would need another man in her life. Still, her intellect and spunk intimidated half the guys she met and her good looks and outdoorsy fitness intimidated the other half. *"Wonder how long this one will last,"* he mused.

He practiced his stern face while he waited for them to appear, standing back under a Palo Verde tree just out of view of the path. He did not have too long to wait. Shelley came into sight with her usual bounce and skip, and then ran back to her companion, only to turn and run ahead again.

Whoa! Roy had not seen her this bouncy since she was fourteen. Something out of the ordinary was in the wind. On her next foray, she saw his truck, and he clearly heard the "Oh-oh."

He stepped out from behind the tree, stern face in place, and cleared his throat. She registered the look, then ran and threw her arms around his neck.

Pete came around the corner, and quickly took in the scene. Roy feigned a fierce glare. "So you told me you were safe. Seems you left out a few details."

"I didn't tell any lies, Dad. But, yes, I did leave out a couple of things to try to save you extra stress. This handsome knight saved my life. Pete, get over here and meet my dad."

Pete extended his hand. "Really pleased to meet you, Roy."

Pete's handshake carried confidence and sincerity.

"Hi. … What do you mean 'saved your life'?" Roy replied, giving Shelley a worried, quizzical look.

"It's a bit of a complicated story, Dad," Shelley broke in. "Can we do it over coffee?"

"Okay. You joining us?" he asked Pete casually.

"I'd be delighted, if Shelley can put up with me for yet another hour. But I'd better take my truck. I'm already late for work, and will have to be on my way as soon as traffic is moving again."

With the road blocked in the direction of the Chemulous plant, he could fit in time for a coffee with Roy and Shelley. For that he would chance his supervisor's annoyance.

As Pete walked to his truck, he studied the line of vehicles waiting for the road to clear. He recognized them right away — three flatbeds, each with a double row of vertical stainless steel tanks. *"It's concentrate,"* he thought, *"on the way to the plant"*. He would have a busy day at the spectrometer, once he made it to work.

…

With the road ahead at a standstill, the small restaurant/coffee shop in town was packed, but they managed to get a table for three looking out onto the parking lot. At Roy's urging, Shelley had left her car and gone back into town with him. Roy wanted some time for just the two of them to talk before Pete arrived.

On the way to the coffee shop, Shelley had explained the general overnight situation, and emphasized that Pete had behaved as a perfect gentleman — while never missing a chance to tease. Roy guessed she was leaving out a few details that he probably didn't want to know anyway. He knew she was really a responsible kid — no, a responsible young woman! Definitely a beautiful young woman, and quite taken with her new acquaintance.

When Pete came in, he waved cheerily, grabbed a coffee at the coffee bar, and headed over to join them.

"You look much younger than I had expected," Pete commented, sipping his coffee and trying to suppress a little grin.

"Why is that?" Roy asked.

"Any dad who has had to keep tabs on this girl would have to be tough as nails to avoid an early grave', Pete laughed.

Roy lost his stern face at that, bursting into laughter. "You seem to have pegged her quite accurately."

"Hey Lancelot. Don't push your luck."

"Yes M'Lady."

Roy liked this young man. He had a brash self-confidence, mixed with a wicked sense of humor. He was clearly well read, well educated, thoughtful, and responsible; and appeared as intrigued and generally smitten by her as she was by him.

Pete glanced at his watch. "Wonder how they are coming with that washout? Not that I wouldn't rather stay here, but our plant is down a side road about ten miles past that washout, and my boss will be fit to be tied if I am much later."

"I stopped and talked to the deputy on the way back," Roy replied. "He figured they should have it open about twelve-thirty. It will take at least another half hour after that just to clear the traffic. Think that rust bucket of yours will make it that far?" he asked in mock seriousness.

"Hey, don't make fun of my ride! It doesn't look like much, but the engine and transmission are sound. Had to sell my Honda to help pay my school bills."

"Oh yes. Shelley mentioned you were doing an advanced degree in engineering, after geology as an undergrad. What area?"

"I haven't made a final decision yet. Coming in from undergrad science, I have to play catch up for a bit. My final choice depends on my math results. From my recent experience at Chemulous, it won't be in chemistry! I don't want our kids to have two heads and one leg."

"Our kids? Who's 'our'? Anyone I know?" Shelley piped in.

"Possibly," he replied. I guess I could have said 'my', but last time I checked it still took two. Anyway, I think I'm leaning toward mechanical. I like building stuff and fixing stuff, even that old heap out there."

"Any interest in solar?" Roy asked.

"Yes, That's an area I think needs a lot more investment, both money and ideas. For example, it always baffles me to see huge tracts of desert chewed up, leveled, and fenced off to make a solar farm. And I don't have near the understanding of desert ecology as M'Lady here."

"I share your concern," Roy replied. "We did one large scale project of that type, but Shelley Girl got her oar in, and we figured out how to get the towers in without scraping off all the vegetation. Interesting thing is, we brought in some cattle and some waste organic material. Four years later, the area is a grassland much like it would have been two centuries ago — when the buffalo still roamed this land."

"The cattle love it," Shelley chimed in. "They follow the shadow from the panels all day, so that keeps them moving. They cut the growth down without overgrazing. The shade from the panels helps prevent the sun from killing all of the microorganisms, giving the soil a chance to recover and become more productive. That in turn helps the soil to hold the moisture. It is all part of a natural cycle."

The waiter arrived back. "Refill? Or would you like the lunch menu?"

Roy nodded. "Please. ... My treat," he said to the young people. "Not every day one meets a knight who saves the king's daughter from a water dragon. The fish sticks are not bad."

"Dad, after Pete's campfire-grilled trout, that would be a major downgrade."

"He cooks too?" Roy exclaimed, grinning at Shelley.

"Knight of many talents," she replied happily.

After the lunch, Shelley walked Pete to his truck while Roy surveyed the scene from his table. *"This one might be a keeper,"* he thought.

"Would you like to see our solar site?" she asked Pete as they reached his truck.

"I would like that very much. Tonight I'll probably have to work late to make up for time lost this morning. Tomorrow after four?" "It's a date," she said brightly.

As Pete headed down the road in his old truck, he patted his breast pocket. He had forgotten about the filter from Shelley's camera.

"Sure hope I get time to run this through the spectrometer today. Something fishy is going on, and I want to know what it is."

Chapter 5 — Chemulous

Pete turned off the main highway and down the small packed-dirt side road. On his first visit to Chemulous, he had been surprised that the road was unmarked, except for the "No Exit" sign. No indication that there was a chemical plant there, or anything of a commercial nature. Only the occasional small convoy of flatbed trucks with the steel tanks, or outgoing trucks with the diluted WM-2-4-7-9 or similar coded products, gave any indication that the plant even existed.

The building was small and run down. From the old wooden signs discarded against the inside of the chain-link fence, Pete guessed it might once have made pesticides for the agricultural industry.

"Little need for that now," he thought with a scowl. *"Bad though that was, now they just genetically modify the crops to produce their own pesticides, and we get to eat the same fare as the bugs."*

Pete knew that the big chemical companies and big agribiz companies had spent millions in lobbying and advertising to defeat the state bills that would require labeling of GMOs.

Of course all the industry studies showed that GMOs were perfectly safe! Just like industry-controlled studies and "independent" studies had hidden the dangers of smoking for several decades.

The inside of the plant was equally smelly, dirty, and run down. Only the stainless steel mixing tanks and the water intake that pumped water from the canal looked relatively new. If he had not needed a job so badly to help with his tuition, he would have never accepted the position. At least his lab was reasonably clean, and closed off from the rest of the plant. But he did have to go out to the receiving area to pull his samples from the bar-coded tanks.

With the exception of the supervisor, most of the dozen or so employees spoke Spanish and kept to themselves. From their demeanor, and the way they were treated by the supervisor, Pete guessed they were undocumented workers from south of the border, working for slave wages.

Predictably, the supervisor was less than pleased with Pete's late appearance, but then the supply trucks from south of the border had also been held up by the same washout. Pete volunteered to work late to finish the tests. Since security was on the plant 24/7, Pete could stay as long as necessary, and security would let him out when he was finished.

It was otherwise slow, with no outgoing shipments scheduled. The supervisor was a bit concerned about their newly hired spectrometer operator. Maybe a spot too bright and inquisitive. "Keep a close eye on him," he told the security guard. "I don't want him anywhere near the mixing room or shipping. Most of the rest of the staff are finished for the day, and I don't want him poking around."

It was nearly ten by the time Pete had prepared and run the last sample. He was dog-tired, but he really had to know. The guard had gone to get some coffee in the guard shack. That would give Pete enough time to flush the lens and get the deposit into a sample tube. Once past that step, he could do the rest in under a half hour.

He had the sample in the tube, and Shelley's filter in its case and safely back in his pocket, by the time the guard returned. The tube had that same chemical smell he had noticed in Shelley's hair. That smell brought back the events of the previous evening, sending his mind spinning far from his lab work. *"Hey, pull yourself together,"* he thought, *"or you'll be here all night."*

Twenty-five minutes later, Pete looked at the results with incredulity. He had been expecting some similarity, but not this close. He pulled up the results from some of the earlier samples. Keeping an eye on the guard, who was busy with the sports page, Pete slipped a memory stick into the USB port and dumped the data set to it. Ejecting the stick and slipping it into his pocket, he then erased the last set of test results from the lab computer, and turned to the guard.

"Okay, I'm finally finished. I just have to shut the machines down and I'm ready to go."

Climbing into his old truck, he fired it up, and headed out of the lot. His mind was racing. He hesitated to call Shelley this late, but as he drove by the washout, he finally gave in.

Pulling to the side, he took out his cell, and dialed her number.

"I was hoping you'd call," was her response on the second ring.

"Shell, we have to talk. I analyzed that stuff on your camera filter, and you are not going to believe what I found."
...

Shelley met him at the door before he had a chance to ring. "We need to keep it down. Dad just crashed for the night. He has meetings scheduled bright and early tomorrow. He said to say hello — and goodbye!" She giggled. "Something about not being quite ready to see you across the table at breakfast."

"Knights have to learn perseverance," he replied with a grimace."

"And patience as well," she laughed, giving him a hug and a kiss on the cheek. "Anyway, I want to hear your big news."

She took his hand and led him around the side of the house to a small patio. There they could sit side by side, with heat from an infrared patio heater. "Can I get you something to snack on? We have some good cheese and maybe some sherry or wine."

"That would be super. Roy made sure I was well fed at lunch, and I had my prepared lunch for supper — but that was six hours ago. Sherry would be great. Sherry with Shelley," he added, as she headed for the door.

She stopped mid stride, pivoted and bounced back into his arms. The kiss was warm and lingering. When they finally came up for air, she looked him in the eye.

"Very nice. I liked that. We must do it again some time soon. But at least for now, Shelley is not on the menu — not yet. Great ladies need decorum — and patience too."

She pushed out of his grip, and skipped back to the door. Pete, in what he thought might be a first, was too stunned to get in his usual witty comment. Feeling suddenly a bit weak in the knees, he retreated to the love seat and flopped down.

His blood pressure was almost back to normal when she returned, carrying a small tray of cheese and crackers with two glasses of Sherry. She handed the tray to him to hold while she sat down, and then took it back, resting it across her bare knees. "Help yourself".

"Everything looks delicious. Even the table looks edible," he quipped.

"I told you the table was not on the menu."

"Yes, but you did say 'yet'. And time seems to work funny when I am around you. Past, present, and future all seem to mush up together, to just be now," he said more seriously.

"I did actually say that, didn't I. 'Loose lips sink ships'," she laughed, before popping a piece of cheese into her mouth, and holding her glass up.

"I'll drink to that," he replied, raising his glass to clink hers.

"Okay Sherlock, now out with the big news."

"Do you have a computer we can use? I put the data on this memory stick."

"I have one in my room. When we finish off the rest of this cheese, we can head in. We'll have to be quiet though. Dad's room is just at the end of the hall, and I really don't want to disturb him. And just 'cause you're in my room, don't get any ideas, Lancelot."

"Yet! — I mean, Yes M'Lady," he grinned.

Her room was a delightful mix of little girl, outdoorsy teen, and business-like scientist, one side holding shelves of very-well-used teddy bears, swimming, running, and diving trophies; pictures of softball and soccer teams, pictures of a younger Shelley with her dad, and some goofy teen-girlfriend poses.

On the other side was a neat desk with a computer and two monitors, a small filing cabinet, and neat sets of very professional photos in group frames showing lizards, insects, plants, and birds — clearly tracking changes and interactions in the desert ecosystems.

Between was her carefully made four-poster bed, with a pink flowered coverlet, scattered cushions, and on the wall behind — a single small photo of a serious-faced woman. She would have been extremely good looking, but there was something in her demeanor that detracted from that potential.

While he was still taking in the overall ambiance, Shelley broke in. "Okay, Sherlock. Stop starring at my bed, and get to your work. The computer is logged in and ready to go."

Pete sat down in the single chair and Shelley stood distractingly close behind him. He opened up a spreadsheet, popped the memory stick in the front USB port, and quickly imported the data. He massaged the columns, then ran some averages.

"Okay," he said after a few moments. "Take a look here".

Resting her elbows on his chair back, she leaned her head in close beside his and looked at the screen. "So what am I looking at here."

"Information that, based on my contract, could put me in jail! So we are going to need to keep hush until we can find another way to get this out, where it can't be traced to me.

"So you see this line on the bottom? That's the percentage of each of the ingredients in the sample from your filter."

"Yeuch! No wonder my hair smelled bad!"

"It smells wonderful now," he replied, pulling her long locks across his face.

"Stick to business, Sherlock! What's this other stuff?"

"Each row contains data from a sample pulled from one of our incoming supply tanks. This is the tank code here. This line is the average across the whole shipment."

"And the average is almost identical to the sample from my filter. So...."

"Yes, quite elementary my dear Watson. The conclusion is obvious. That smelly mist that hit you just before the rain came from the Chemulous plant!"

"Chemulous — cumulus. Of course! Cloud seeding, weather modification. So that's what caused the freak storm that nearly killed me!"

"But these chemicals are highly toxic! Barium, arsenic, aluminum, cadmium, chromium, lead. That's crazy! No one in their right mind would deliberately spray that stuff into the environment, would they?" Pete asked.

"'In their right mind' is the operative question. One of the problems of today's technology is that everyone is so specialized that we often miss the 'big picture'."

"And when large companies or governments get involved in projects, information sharing becomes very restricted — even information from academic sources you should be able to trust. Lots of non-disclosure documents like the one you had to sign. Along with lots of money changing hands.

"And yes," she continued, "most of these are highly toxic, even in fairly low concentrations. But even worse is that they tend to concentrate the higher up the food chain you go. For example, plants like rice will concentrate toxins like arsenic. If cattle eat crops containing toxins, and we then eat the cattle, the effects are multiplied."

"I have read stuff online about large-scale weather modification experiments," Pete replied, "but governments have always dismissed it as 'crackpot conspiracy theory'. Yet in other places, some prominent people have openly advocated dumping crap into the atmosphere to combat global warming."

"Yes," she said, "these people are the real crackpots. They have no clue what the long-term effects might be. But you can bet there's a good buck to be made."

"I need to find out more about what is going on at Chemulous," Pete replied. "I have copied the files back to my stick, so you can delete them from your computer."

"I think I should keep a copy for now. But we really need to be careful. There are possibly interests behind this who could be dangerous."

"We? I started this, and am in the middle, because of my job. I don't want you in more danger. I already saved you once remember. That's enough excitement for a while."

Shelley shook her head. "No way Sherlock. For my thesis, I have been working on the unexplained decline of some lizard and toad species that are really important to the health of the entire desert ecosystem. I suspected something toxic in the environment. I'm guessing this weather manipulation might be part of the answer. Besides, isn't saving damsels in distress what knights do?"

Pete stood and turned to her, wrapped his arms around her waist, and starred seriously into her eyes, before replying. "Yes, it is in the job description. But if anything happened to you, I could not forgive myself."

"Ditto. So we have to watch each other's backs."

This time he initiated the kiss, to a clearly positive response. After a moment he pulled away to gaze at her again.

"M'Lady's charms are disintegrating my shields, and tempting me away from chivalrous conduct. Methinks I had best fire up my iron steed and beat a hasty retreat while there is yet time."

"Yet — I mean yes," she replied with a bright smile. They took another few minutes to say goodnight at the door, before Pete climbed somewhat reluctantly into his truck and drove from the yard.

Chapter 6 — Dimming Dawn

Shelley spent the morning working on a project for RoySolar. It was around eleven when she went out to the site, climbing the hill to retrieve the data from the sensors arrayed there.

As she started back down the hill, she noticed two flatbeds approaching on the highway. Each had two rows of shiny cylindrical metal tanks sitting vertically on the flatbed. Based on Pete's description, she wondered if these might be supply trucks for Chemulous.

Removing her Nikon from her pack, she zoomed in as close as she could get, and took a brief burst of multiple photos. The tanks were held in place by double strands of steel cable. These were passed through fittings that were welded to the tanks a ways up from the bottom and down from the top. She would ask Pete about them when he arrived for the site tour just after four.

She was sure she had seen trucks just like this somewhere else, but she couldn't remember where. Maybe it would come back to her. Meanwhile she had to get her latest sensor data into her laptop. Might as well put the photos on her laptop too. But first she was supposed to meet Roy in the project trailer that served as a lunchroom for the site staff.

She arrived first, put her pack on one of the small tables, and went to the fridge to get the lunch she had prepared. She was just organizing the food when Roy came in.

"Hi Dad. How did your meetings go?"

He gave her a hug. "Not too bad. Some of the investors are a bit antsy due to those reports of 'global dimming'. Seems there is not a fully natural explanation, what with lowered levels of industrial pollution in this part of the world. We are south of stuff that is coming over from China.

"But global dimming still seems to be getting worse, particularly here in the southwest, and it will definitely impact our solar output numbers. Which of course makes it harder to compete with fossil fuel. Seems like a vicious circle".

"Would it at least have the effect of slowing global warming?"

"Well that's what the proponents of geoengineering claim, but their thinking sure seems simple-minded to me. Sure we can spend billions dumping gunk into the atmosphere, with no idea of how to get rid of it again if it doesn't do the job they think it will. And that gunk will reflect some of the energy back to space.

"But the earth itself already does that. Which is why it gets so bloody cold out here in the desert at night. When there is a cloud layer, the heat loss is much lower. The chemicals would be expected to do much the same thing. So the net effect could be negative — especially if it affects the various frequencies of light differently. And that is without factoring in the effects on crops and oxygen-generating plant life if we reduce the natural solar flux. Much too risky from my perspective.

" ... So you expecting Pete today?," he asked, deftly changing the subject.

"Yes, I am, sometime after four, when he is off work. I was explaining how the cattle worked symbiotically with the tracking solar, and offered to show him around. How did you know?"

Roy chuckled. "Well, for a start, you dumped your usual faded tee and grubby work jeans for your fanciest blouse and shortest shorts. And then there is the time you obviously spent on your hair. Taken together, those might be seen as a bit of a give away. You don't generally dress like that for the construction crew or the ageing consultants you work with. ... You look smashing by the way."

Shelley flashed him a smile. "Well you do like him, don't you?"

Roy smiled back, and then turned more serious, a shadow darkening his face.

"Yes, I like him. He seems like a nice young man. But you and I know from first hand experience that not all is what it seems."

Shelley nodded. She knew the torment and the betrayal that Roy felt — and that she felt — when his wife, her mother, essentially 'shacked up' with her French instructor, shortly before announcing she was leaving for an overseas posting and wanted a divorce.

"Just be careful, Shelley. I don't want you hurt."

"It is a little late for that," she thought. "I'm already hooked, and if it falls apart with Pete, it is going to hurt big time." "I'll be careful," she replied.

They ate in silence after that. As he stood to go, he put his big hand on her shoulder. "Shelley Girl, you have no idea how much I want this to work for you. For all that Jane put me through, she did give me you, and for that I will be eternally grateful to her. "Say hi to Pete for me."

After Roy left, Shelley cleaned up the lunch remains, and headed for her office in trailer two. She fired up her laptop, logged into the network, and transferred the sensor data. Then she pulled the memory card from her camera, and loaded the photos. She did not take time to look at them yet, as she wanted to follow up on Roy's "global dimming" comment.

After two hours of following her nose on the Internet, her head was spinning. Yes, there were some 'crackpots' out there, and some most improbable conspiracy theories. But there was also a steady drip of real information, real data, and highly credible people suggesting a massive but largely invisible intervention in the world climate system - not in some future time, but right now, and for possibly decades in the past!

She had dumped Pete's spreadsheet data on a stick, and that gave her a whole new avenue to explore. The links led down more alleys. Then she hit real pay dirt!

The loud knock on the door pulled her out of her plunge. She opened the door. Pete stepped in, looked around to ensure they were alone, and pulled her into an embrace.

She surrendered to the impulse momentarily, with immense pleasure, but then pulled away. "Hold on Romero. We have some serious business to attend to. You have to look at what I found. It will blow your mind. No time for hanky-panky. Not yet, anyway."

"I'm coming to have a thing about that 'yet' word," Pete replied, as Shelley pretty much dragged him to her workstation.

"Me too. But there is something very important for you to see, before you get distracted. You know that chemical signature you got from my filter? I've found not one, but two matches on the web!"

"I'm always distracted when I'm near you, so it is too late to avoid that problem. We will just have to work around it. Okay Watson, what have you turned up in your investigation?"

She showed him the links.

"Hold it. So you're telling me that the chemical signature we found is consistent with the measured increase in toxic substances in California drinking water over ten years, and also with the measured values of hazardous waste from a former industrial-military site in New Mexico? That makes no sense!"

"Doesn't it?" Shelley returned. "Suppose a company could get a big contract for hazardous waste cleanup, turning huge profits, and could then minimally process it before talking another part of government into spraying it into the atmosphere — to get rid of it — while making even bigger profits?"

"Come on! That is too far fetched! The CEO of such a company would have to be a psychopath!"

"Yes, he would. And according to recent research, there are possibly four times as many CEOs who are psychopaths as is common in the rest of the population. Seems it is a desirable trait in senior managers of companies that care only about profits."

"Now of course," she added, "it would require employees who were either complicit in the scheme, or lacked sufficient visibility into the overall operation to know what was going on. Then there are twenty-page employment contracts threatening years in the pen if you spill the beans. All of those would play a part."

"Whoa. I need some time to digest all of this. ... But now that I think about it, my direct supervisor certainly fits the profile. He abuses the Spanish-speaking workers unmercifully. He drives a Mercedes convertible, and seems to have a different floozy in the car with him every week. I have little doubt he would poison half the world if it meant a better car and a higher class hooker."

"Don't the workers push back," she asked?

"No, not directly. My guess is that most are undocumented, and complaining would get them a quick appointment with the immigration folks, and a bus ticket back south of the border."

"You are probably right about that," she replied. "Speaking of Chemulous, I took some pictures this morning I wanted to ask you about. I haven't really looked closely at them myself. There's a whole series here. ... So are these the type of trucks you referred to?"

"Certainly looks like them. Yes, that looks identical. You sure took a lot of the same or similar shots."

"Sorry about that. I take mainly wildlife photos, so always have the camera on burst mode. Four shots per second."

"Okay, just a bit repetitive. But these are definitely our trucks. ... Whoa! There is something weird there! Back up one. Forward again. Okay. See that space in between the last four tanks?"

"Yes, what about it? Looks the same as the others."

"Okay, now go back to the previous frame, and zoom in on that same spot."

"You're right! They are not the same! What is it?"

"Elementary, my dear Watson. An undocumented worker is stretching his cramped legs — hidden between the tanks and hidden from x-rays by the tanks themselves. So that truck must have come from Mexico!"

"That's it," Shelley broke in. "I knew I had seen those trucks before. I spent a couple of weeks doing fieldwork a ways East of Yuma. There was a little-used border crossing on a dirt road about five miles to the south of where I was working. I remembered because the big trucks seemed so out of place on that narrow road."

"And you said that hazardous waste site was in New Mexico? Watson, I'm going to have to give you a raise."

Chapter 7 — Commitment?

Shelley mulled over what she and Pete had learned the previous day. The big question was how to get the information out there without getting Pete in legal trouble.

He had suggested that one of his profs in Tucson might be willing to run an independent analysis of the residue from the filter. What happened with the mist on that mountaintop was not tied to his agreement.

Shelley also had a trusted girlfriend who knew an investigative reporter personally. Between those two independent people, they thought there might be a way to expose this criminal activity.

Pete was going down to Tucson early in the next week, and would take the filter with him. That would be a spot lonely for her, she was certain. They had managed at least some time together every day during the week, even with their respective jobs. But today was Saturday, so they had decided to go back up to the canyon where they had met, and spend the night.

As she dressed and packed, she momentarily wondered if she was really ready for "Yet". She stopped and was very still within herself. Then she smiled, reached in the drawer for her second most outrageously frilly undies, and threw them in her pack. The others were already on.

They hadn't discussed 'yet' in the context of the weekend, but she was confident he would respect her decision either way. *"Though he would have an obvious preference,"* she thought with a little giggle. She grabbed her camera gear, and headed down stairs.

Roy had breakfast on. "So you're gone until tomorrow night?" he asked casually. Shelley nodded. "You're my twenty-five year old little Shelley Girl, so no lectures are needed. Not that you always paid attention in the past."

She grinned, and gave him a hug. "Oh I paid attention, but I thought I knew better. Turned out your radar was better than mine. Both times they were jerks. It just took me longer to figure it out."

"Well at least nothing more serious happened. Some girls end up with a little reminder of their rebellion against their all-knowing father. Anyway, if my radar is still working correctly, this one is not a jerk. ... Not that I think you want any 'little' reminders of this particular weekend either," he added hastily.

Shelley laughed. "No worries on that score Dad."

As she ate, it occurred to her how difficult it must have been for Roy — having her mom walk out on him, just as Shelley was entering those critical years. He had been forced to deal with her feminine issues along with everything else — all of those little 'talks' that most girls would take to their mums. She leaned over and kissed him on the forehead.

"What was that for," he asked.

"Just for being you, and always being there for me — and for having accurate radar."

Pete picked her up around ten-thirty. She had offered to take her car, but he pointed out that his old crate was less likely to get broken into if left at the trail head overnight. They were at the parking lot by shortly after eleven.

Grabbing their gear, they headed up into the first canyon. Everywhere the desert was in bloom. It seemed to Pete that Shelley photographed every tree, yucca, prickly pear, every bird and crawly thing, to say nothing of dozens of pictures of him, and several taken with the timer of the both of them. Interspersed with picture taking, and her skips, hops, and bounces, there were the numerous times she bounced into his arms for a long kiss.

Then there were his excursions to explain the geology of the region, and to search the canyon wall for probable sources of the polished rose quartz, turquoise, and pyrite that Shelley spotted at intervals in the bed of the wash.

Taken together, these activities added probably three hours to the journey. He smiled to himself as she skipped ahead for the fiftieth time to investigate something new that caught her eye. Yes, it was taking extra time, but her joy of life was extremely contagious. He could not imagine a more fun day. Even when her attempts to teach him to skip met with mixed success!

They lunched on a big rock, while she explained the habits of the towhee. "Now there's a lesson in that, Lancelot," she said in mock seriousness.

In another hour, they reached the bottom of the wash, and could see the small ledge above. The cave was not visible from where they stood. Shelley stopped and gazed at the splintered wood and scattered rocks littering the wash.

"That shattered branch could have been me," she thought.

"So right there you saved my life. Now it will take me a whole lifetime to pay you back."

"Sounds like a deal to me. Lancelot gets the princess, and they live happily ever after. At least for the rest of their lives."

She gave him a hug, and took time for only a quick peck, before spinning away again. "Better get with it Lancelot. My royal quarters must be prepared, my royal fire made, and my royal supper cooked. Chop-chop!"

They spent the next hour working side by side, gathering and breaking wood, laying out their things in the small cave, supporting the tarp to provide cover from the night chill, and unpacking the food supplies.

"You didn't bring a sleeping bag, it seems. Was that an oversight?" Pete asked.

"No. Not an oversight. Since this is the six-day anniversary of your act of heroism, I thought we should recreate the conditions and experience as closely as possible."

"As closely as possible?" he echoed, a certain uncertainty and disappointment in his voice.

Shelley turned away to hide the grin. "As possible," she intoned. "I did, however, allow for the fact you might find it difficult to find a fresh Trout, so I packed one in.

"But I do expect it to be cooked with the same degree of culinary excellence. Some small deviations might be permitted in other areas".

"Such as a water substitute?" Pete asked, producing a bottle of Champagne wrapped in damp towels from his pack.

"Hmmm. I don't know. My father warned me about strange men attempting to ply me with liquor. ... Oh, what the heck. It is our six-day anniversary, after all. Ply away Lancelot!"

He produced two wine glasses from his pack, opened the bottle, and poured them each a glass. "To the most beautiful princess in the Kingdom," he toasted.

"And to her heroic, faithful, and dedicated Knight, Lancelot. Oh! Did I mention handsome!" She replied.

"Thank you, M'Lady."

"Oh, yes, and overly optimistic! This princess holds her booze pretty well — even champagne."

Pete laughed. Then he poked at the remains of their previous fire, pulling out the larger charcoal pieces.

"I need to get the fire started, or we are going to be eating trout sushi and freezing M'Lady's pretty butt — speaking of which, a leather gown to cover thy beautiful legs is wrapped in blue tissue in my pack."

Shelley smiled, inclined her head, curtsied, and disappeared into the cave. She found the blue tissue, and pulled the leather out. She gasped in surprise. It was not Pete's rock skin, but a beautiful fringed and beaded skirt of doeskin!

Even in the dim light of the cave, she could see that the native craftsmanship was remarkable. She pressed it to her face, savoring the rich soft texture and smell of natural leather. Then she pulled off her shorts, and slipped the skirt over her frilly undies. *"Definitely a better match with these panties,"* she thought.

When she emerged from the cave, Pete appraised her carefully. She stepped into his waiting arms. "A small deviation," he said with a smile. She kissed him so hard he almost lost his balance.

"I gather an acceptable one," he ventured. Before she could reply she was convulsed with laughter. On the rock above he had quickly filled in the rock art to complete the picture where her clothes had once served that function.

"I call it 'Adam and Eve' he quipped. "But I couldn't find any fig leaves."

"You're awful," she hooted, holding her stomach.

By the time he had the fire started, she almost had her giggles under control — as long as she didn't look in that direction.

The fish was excellent, and paired well with the champagne, and the veggies she had packed. As the stars came out and the moon appeared over the adjacent peak, they cuddled under a blanket and stared silently into the fire. Pete had produced two small lanterns containing candles that cast a soft glow, adding to the ambiance.

As the fire collapsed in a flurry of sparks, Pete kissed her gently on the cheek. "Time for bed, M'Lady."

She nodded. "This has been the most wonderful evening of my life," she replied. "Can we take the candles in?"

"Minor deviation. We didn't have candles last time."

"Or champagne," she replied.

Pete stood up and stirred the fire. Then he pointed to the far end of the ledge. "And mind that leather," he cautioned.

"You can be assured of that. It is way too beautiful to get soiled."

When she ducked into the cave, Pete had placed the candles in the lower spaces next to the wall. He held up her discarded shorts. "Another deviation," he commented. "Should I put them in your pack?"

"Not really a deviation," she corrected, "except they were wet last time. But this is," she continued, raising the leather skirt just enough to reveal the red frills below. "Definitely a better match for this beautiful skirt than those cotton boxers of yours, don't you think? ... Oh yes, before you put those shorts away, there is something in the right pocket for you, Lancelot."

He withdrew the small packets and starred at them, almost in disbelief.

"Yes, 'yet' is now, or at least imminent, my Knight. Just make sure you use them as directed when the time comes."

"M'Lady honors me too highly," he replied with a smile so broad she was afraid his face would break. She relieved that smiling stress by kissing him deeply.

"I did say 'recreate the experience as closely as possible', so let's get close before we get too cold. With the sleeping bag spread out this way, hypothermia could set in fast."

"Now if I remember correctly, I think the next step was getting Jeeves to remove my boots." She unbuttoned her shirt, and then wiggled back into the low space to bring her feet within reach.

She felt him untie the laces, remove the boots and socks, and then she felt his lips caress the top of her foot.

"Mistress Shelley's beautiful feet are warmer than last time."

"So you won't threaten to keep me out of the sleeping bag this time," she laughed.

"Not really the slightest chance of that."

"Well since you are down there anyway, and last time you frequently offered help, maybe I'll take you up on it this time. You could help with this."

She undid the fastening and lifted her hips, pushing the skirt down. He pulled it gently over her feet, and then sat up to fold it carefully and set it on her pack. He then resumed his position, and she felt his hands and lips caress up her legs to the thigh. She raised her hips again, and felt the frilly silk slide down and off. His lips continued their upward journey.

She inhaled loudly, and felt her body respond. She thought of Paulo Coehlo's book, "Eleven Minutes". Her previous experiences had been definitely of the "slam, bam, thank you ma'am" variety. Pete seemed in no particular hurry. She lay almost still, absorbing this new sensation. She had no idea if it was seconds or minutes before she broke the silence.

"Yo, Lancelot. Most pleasant as that feels, there is more of me up here to explore, some of which is getting a little chilly, in spite of the overall effect you are having on my metabolism."

"Sorry M'Lady. The roof is low, and I seem to be stuck."

"Likely story," she giggled, before taking a couple of deep gasps as he returned to his task. "Okay, I better slide down before I use up all the air in this narrow space."

She felt him lift his weight, and 'graze' upward on her abdomen as she wiggled back out of the crevice.

"And what is this strange silken garment that encumbers thy beautiful bod."

"It hooks in front — more suited for low ceilings," she giggled.

"How thoughtful of those designers," he replied, undoing the clasp, and continuing his exploration.

"Hmmm. Yes it was, wasn't it? You seem to have run into another obstacle, or distraction."

"Two of them actually. The most admirable of distractions."

"Well shed those duds, get things organized, and then finish your exploration. I'm ready for 'as close as possible'".

Chapter 8 — Stowaway

Shelley awoke as the sun was just coming over the mountain. Extricating herself from the tangle of limbs without fully waking Pete took a moment, and came with a definite reluctance, but her bladder was not about to be denied. She threw a windbreaker over her upper half, leaving the lower half to fend for itself in the crisp desert air.

Scurrying back in and closing the tarp behind her, she discovered a not so sleepy hand appraising her bare derriere.

"M'Lady has a somewhat chilled but very pretty butt. Methinks this situation could be improved by the application of the survival principle of shared body heat, should she be so inclined."

"Best not to chance hypothermia, Lancelot. So I'll take you up on your kind offer, if you're properly prepared and up to the task."

"Quite up for the task M'Lady. Fully prepared for boarding, so to speak."

She peeled off the windbreaker, opened the sleeping bag and bounced on top of him. "Take no prisoners me hearties." It took almost no time to raise her temperature.

She awoke for the second time to find Pete gone. The flap was partially up, and the smell of wood smoke filled the air. Only moments later, Pete appeared with a streaming cup of coffee.

She reached up and wrapped her arms around his neck. Resting the hot coffee to one side, he responded to the invitation. He marveled at his own response. He had kissed many girls over the years, but none came even close to this experience. His entire being seemed to soar into a different realm of color and sensation. He pulled back to look into her mischievous eyes.

"No, no M'Lady. Temptress that you are, I must return to my duties. Or be yet in this enchanted land for fifty years."

"Sounds good to me," she responded.

"Would that I could, but honor and duty calls. Tomorrow I must ride my trusty (and rusty) steed to the Kingdom of Tucson, where we will slay the Chemulous dragon."

"Thou art so heroic, what can a princess say?"

She pushed back the sleeping bag, reached for the coffee, and stepped out into the sunshine. Like some ancient priestess, she stood in nakedness to address the four sacred directions, as Pete followed her every movement. Then she turned to face him, bowed briefly, and returned to the cave. She emerged in the doeskin skirt, with a towel pinned shawl-like round her shoulders.

"So where is my breakfast, Jeeves? And do try not to be distracted."

...

They packed up the camp before heading out on the mesa. They arrived at the point, looking down nearly five hundred feet, to where the main road ran west to east. The sun beat down, and the updrafts stirred the grasses and low shrubs that covered the mesa.

"Great spot for an all-over tan," she observed. She had already shed the 'shawl' from the top half as the sun climbed higher.

"Indeed my lady, though you put the sun to shame."

She kissed him, and then dropped her skirt to the ground. "You are quick of tongue, Lancelot, but your lady had relaxing undisturbed in mind. You are welcome to join me in the sun worship ceremony, but you must keep your energies appropriately focused. To put it more bluntly, no hanky-panky! Besides, I packed only three sheaths for your sword, and by my count we seem to have used them all up."

"M'Lady seems to have forgotten I was a boy scout. Our motto was 'be prepared'."

She had of course expected as much, but had not been ready to take that chance.

"Always the optimist. Forget it Lancelot. Sun worship only! Now do thy duty and spend this sunscreen in appropriate places, including my pretty butt."

"With the utmost of pleasure, M'Lady."

"Yes, and equally of extreme pleasure to the princess," she thought to herself. *"Win-win."*

They spread the sleeping bag on the rock, and Shelley lay on her stomach.

She luxuriated under his touch, and soon dozed in the warm rays of the sun.

"Best turn that beautiful bod, M'Lady, lest you fry to a crisp."

She rolled onto her back and reached for the sunscreen. "Jeeves can be of assistance?" he asked hopefully.

Shelley laughed. "I could do this side myself, you know. You don't always have to wait on me hand and foot ... and other places ... as much as I seem to enjoy being waited on. You managed your front quarters yourself, while I lazed in the sun. Roll over and let me do your back ... and other places."

As she worked, she noted the lean but supple muscles. *"Petty solid guy, both inside and out. This one I'll keep,"* she thought to herself. *"And about time I got lucky."*
"Okay, Lancelot. All done. Set your timer, and relax."

He hitched up his knees and sat back on his heels, extending his hand for the lotion. "You wouldn't deprive a Knight of his simple pleasures, would you, my beautiful princess?"

She laughed and handed him the bottle, which he received with a broad smile. It was quite an oily preparation, and she noted how his body gleamed in the bright desert sun.

He started at her forehead and worked to her toes. She came close to losing her resolve more than once. Of course, the fact that he insisted on kissing and/or nibbling each spot on her body before liberally applying and working in the oily lotion probably had something to do with that.

But she held out until he finished with the sunscreen and was once again face down on the sleeping bag. After another few minutes of cooking, she sat up and rifled through her pack, pulling out the clean undies, a shirt and shorts. As she began dressing, Pete rolled on one elbow and watched the progress.

"Have I died and gone to heaven, pretty angel?"

"Of course. All angels wear frilly red underwear, right?"

"Well mine does it seems, and wears it most wonderfully."

"Come make yourself useful. This one fastens in the back."

He stood and took her in his arms, reaching round behind her to take the bra straps.

"Hey there Lancelot, you are supposed to be doing that up, not taking it off again!"

"Oh yes, that's right. Darn. Oh well. Another time perhaps?" he asked, as he clipped the straps in place.

"I think that's highly likely," she replied. "Too bad you are away all next week."

"Yes, but perhaps you could come down to Tucson for a bit."

"I might talk my slave driver boss into that. ... I think Roy really likes you, as hard as it is for him to give up his little girl to another man. I hope your parents approve of trollops in red panties."

"My mother," he corrected. "My dad was killed in a accident a few years back. It was hard for a while, but my mom is a very positive and resilient type of person. And she'll positively adore you. I'll get the 'don't screw up and lose her' lecture for sure," he laughed.

"Sounds like Pete's mother is a lot like Roy," she thought.

"Have you 'screwed up and lost her' before?" she asked with curiosity.

"Well, sort of. Mother liked the particular 'her', and she was a 'nice' girl if you know the type. Not a lot of spunk. Rather low energy. We really weren't a 'match' at all. She saw me with another girl one day, and flipped her lid. Mother was a bit upset — something about wanting grandchildren before she was too old. Anyway, it was obviously predestined — so I could meet you," he added.

"Well take your mom's advice on this one Lancelot, and don't screw up. No snogging with any other princesses." He looked at her aghast. "M'Lady must believe me when I tell her that I have no interest in other women."

Shelley was about to come back with a funny comment when she became aware of movement on the road below.

"Pete, isn't that a Chemulous truck down there?"

He turned to gaze down at the roadway, while she grabbed her camera. As they watched, the truck pulled over to the shoulder. The driver walked to the front of the rig and appeared to relieve himself, then leaned against the truck and lit up a cigarette.

Just as she focused her telephoto lens on the rig, a figure appeared, slowly climbing out from the space between the last four tanks. He moved to the outside of the truck, and then jumped. As he hit the ground, his leg seemed to give out, and he limped into the low bush bordering the road.

The driver finished his cigarette, climbed into the cab, and the rig moved back into the road. As the truck accelerated away to the east, they saw the figure emerge from the bushes and head towards the canyon. He made it about a hundred yards before collapsing in a heap.

"Pete, that man is in big trouble! Get that bod of yours into some clothes, and let's move. It will take at least an hour to get down, and judging from the way he was behaving, he will do well to last that long."

R.A. Abell

Chapter 9 — Undocumented

It took well over an hour for Pete and Shelley to get down to the bottom of the canyon, moving as quickly as they could over the difficult ground. They spotted the man prostate on the ground in the partial shadow of a large rock.

Shelley noted he was farther up the trail from the spot where she had seen him fall, and from the marks on the ground it appeared he had crawled here in an attempt to get out of the sun. She grabbed a water bottle from her pack, and checked his pulse and breathing.

"Well, he's still alive, but his skin is burning up. He is very dehydrated and obviously suffering from heat exhaustion. Do you have extra water in the truck?"

Pete replied in the affirmative. He always kept a full jerrycan of drinking water, just in case his old truck broke down in the desert.

"We don't need it just yet. It can be dangerous to give him too much water right away. But see if you can sit him up against the rock, and we'll try to get a bit of water into him. Then maybe you can use the tarp to provide more shade. After that will be soon enough for you to get the other water. I want it mainly to get his skin temperature down."

As they tried to prop him up, he partially opened his eyes, raised one hand to a crucifix at his throat, and mumbled incoherently in Spanish. Shelley dampened a small towel and ran it over his face and neck.

Then she put the water bottle to his parched lips, being careful to not let him have too much at a time. Pete rigged the tarp to provide shade, and then headed for the truck. Shelley continued to use the towel to cool the man's skin.

He was very dark skinned; short and stocky, and dressed like the typical Mexican laborer. Probably around forty years old. She wondered how long he had been hiding in the truck. Since it was almost three now, he would have suffered through the intense heat for hours, with the sun overhead reflecting from the tank walls to the very bottom of his hiding spot.

Shelley knew that dozens of so-called "illegals" died in the desert every year, trying to get into the U.S. Once there, the best they could hope for would be a very low-paying laboring job, usually picking for unscrupulous companies who regularly abused their workers and frequently violated safety rules and regulations.

She knew that her Dad insisted on vetting all of his subcontractors to ensure they followed the rules. Roy also directly employed a couple of trusted Mexican workers who had the proper documentation and lived in a trailer at the work site.

She again raised the water bottle to his parched lips, allowing him a little more each time. He opened his eyes again, and this time seemed to recognize where he was. He smiled weakly, and put a shaky hand on her arm.

"Mucho Gracias, Señorita. I theenk you save my life."

"We were very worried we might not get to you in time. We saw you from up there," she said, pointing to the mesa area extending toward the road like a long broad finger.

She gave him another small sip of water. "You must not drink too much at once, she cautioned. ... Why did you get out of the truck here?"

"Eet was first time zee truck stop since border. I run out water before even get zhere. I not know so far!"

She gave him another sip, and wiped his face with the towel, which was now almost too dry to be useful. Then she saw Pete's truck coming toward them, making slow but steady progress over the rugged terrain.

"I feel dizzy in head," he continued. "When truck stop, think I see angel, telling me get out of zee truck now! ... I think I find real angel, Señorita," he smiled, his brown eyes showing a bit more life.

He started and tensed at the sudden sound of the approaching truck, then relaxed as Pete's old jalopy bounced into view.

"Just my friend Pete. He has more water in the truck. Good thing, because this towel doesn't have much cooling anymore. And it will be easier to get you out of here as well." She wasn't sure just where they would go from here, but first things first.

"Peete?

"Yes, and my name is Shelley."

"I am Rafael Rodriguez Sanchez Garcia. Mucho Gracious, Señorita Angel Shelley."

"She is an angel, isn't she? Glad to see you looking better," Pete commented, as he came up to the improvised shelter. "I'm Pete."

Shelley took the towel and soaked it liberally from the jerrycan, running the cooling water over Rafael's back and chest. She didn't worry about getting the shirt wet, as that would continue the cooling effect for a longer time. She then started to wipe down the lower leg and ankle on his right side.

He winced and grunted in pain. *"Oh-oh,"* she thought, *"another complication."*

She handed the towel to Pete. "I should have remembered that Rafael stumbled when he jumped. Take over the water duties, while I check out this ankle."

She started a careful examination from the knee down, watching her patient's reaction and asking about the pain as she went.

"Do you think it's broken?" Pete asked.

"No, I'm almost certain it's just a sprain — which is a really good thing! It should heal itself without a doctor's intervention. You are going to have to stay off this leg for a week or so!" she said to Rafael.

"Given that Rafael is probably undocumented, having to take him to a hospital would be a major problem," she thought to herself."

"But I must find job!" he replied, with a very distressed look.

"My wife and family, they in danger. I need to move zhem from village. ... Very soon," he added. "To move, need money".

"Right now you need to get out of here. We'll take you to Dad's construction site. I think he will find a way to help. Pete, put that wet towel around Rafael's ankle to help keep it from swelling more than it has already, and let's get him into the truck."

When he finished securing the towel, Pete took Rafael's right side to support the sprained ankle, and Shelley the left. They got him into the cab on the passenger side, and headed back to load the supplies.

"You seemed to know exactly what you were doing Shelley Nightingale."

"I should. I spent seven years as a camp counselor. Had to recert First Aid every year."

"Handy skills for a mother," he mused. "So what do you make of his comment about his family being in danger?"

"Well," she replied, "I think he is sincere, and genuinely worried. Since he arrived on a Chemulous truck, it would not surprise me if there is a connection. Maybe we can find out what is going on at the other end of the pipeline."

Rafael was much better, but did still have a headache — not an unusual symptom after heat exhaustion. Pete's old clunker was equipped with an air conditioning system that actually still worked, so they were able to keep the cab at a suitable temperature during the trip.

As curious as she was, Shelley didn't want to push Rafael to talk, but he was very concerned about the border patrol, and wanted them to understand his predicament. He explained that most of the people in his town were having health problems of one sort or another. In recent years, the older people were dying of cancers, including his parents.

Many children did not survive childbirth, died in infancy, or were born with defects. The men who worked in the plant were the worst, seeming to be always sick. The company had to bring in more workers from other towns just to keep the plant working. One of these new men had quietly complained to the local authorities, and was found shot two days later.

Rafael made the sign indicating bribery. "Zhere ees no one help us. Zee company run by very bad men! I farming, but now crops dying. Zee water from well taste bad. Air smell bad all time. When I try send peppers California, zhey not let in — say 'contaminated'. So I want move my family to Los Algodones. Have sister there, works for dentist. She get me small land near town. I can farm."

"So why didn't you just move?" Shelley asked, "rather than take that awful chance sneaking across the border? You almost died, which would not have helped your family at all."

"Took all money to buy new land. Need 25,000 pesos to get moving truck. No one wants buy land near village, so I decide try work U.S. long enough to pay moving."

"This plant you mentioned; what does it do?" Pete asked. "Is that where the truck that you hid on came from?"

"Si, Señor. Zee trucks leave each day. Sometimes take workers North, to work in plant up here. So I hide same place. Driver no know I zhere."

"Zee plant work on garbage. First, just — how you say — 'landfill' — cans, bottles, car battery. Truck come every day. From east. Soon, want to make bigger, but Federales say no! So zhey build plant, burn, use water from creek to wash, then bury. Water go out in truck like I on."

"So that explains some of it," Pete mused. "Somebody important downstream — probably an agribiz — must have complained to get the Federales involved. So the owners turned their problem into a business opportunity. Wash some of the worst stuff out, and export it again as a 'chemical mix'. That would explain the large variation from batch to batch. What they bury affects only the local village, so spreading a little money to local officials solves their problem."

"But wouldn't all that effort cost more than it's worth?" Shelley asked.

"Depends on where the original waste is coming from," he replied. "State and Federal agencies pay out some very significant change to contractors to clean up hazardous waste sites. One big site can be a five to ten year project. If the contractor could then find a way to make more money on the other end...."

"We're going to have to get Roy involved in this," Shelley mused as they drove into the solar site. "He has some good contacts, and might have some ideas on how to proceed."

R.A. Abell

Chapter 10 — Plan to Action

Roy sat at the lunchroom table, considering the scenario that Shelley and Pete had laid out. It seemed bizarre, but he had seen a lot in his day. Anything was possible. His shareholders had expressed a concern about global dimming.

At the same time, there were increasingly frequent suggestions that blocking sunlight would be a technological solution to global warming, often by the same interests who claimed global warming was a hoax.

That unscrupulous companies would push these wacky ideas as a ticket to riches would not be surprising. The fact that they could do irreversible damage to the environment and violence to hundreds, thousands, or millions would be of no consequence to them.

Then there was Rafael. He would have to go back to Mexico. Roy had housed him temporarily with his other Mexican workers and drivers. They were all properly documented, and had been trained in handling and installing panels, or drove the rigs carrying materials to the site. Rafael could not help with that work, even if he had the papers. Not with that ankle.

"Okay" Roy began. "Let's start with Rafael. He needs to get back home, and we need to keep him out of the hands of the border patrol. They would probably just dump him back over the border. I have heard from reliable sources on the Mexican side that the border patrol often moves these unfortunate people many miles away from their entry point."

"That's horrible!" Shelley exclaimed.

"Yes, it is. Maybe just administrative, or maybe intended to 'teach them a lesson'. As a nation, we can be quite capable of inhumanity. Especially with people whose skin is a different shade."

"They really do that?" Pete asked incredulously.

"My source was an officer in the Mexican police. He had no reason to lie. He told me that people caught in the Yuma area have been taken as far as Tijuana and dumped there with no money, no food, and no way to get home."

"The Border Patrol makes sure they are fed and get water while inside the U.S., but once they are unloaded from the bus and herded across the border, they are on their own. Apparently there is some informal volunteer group in Mexico that helps out. So it must happen too often to just be some occasional rogue field officer in the border patrol."

"It does sound like 'policy', doesn't it?" Pete replied.

"So what are you thinking, Dad?" Shelley asked.

"Well, I was planning to send a truck down to pick up some aluminum racking from my Mexican supplier on Wednesday. That would allow three days for Rafael's sprain to heal. The patrol never worries about southbound traffic, and my driver has all the right paperwork."

"So it would not be that big a deal for the truck to make a side trip to deliver Rafael back home. I wish I could do more, but cash flow is tight at this point in the project, so I really am not comfortable just giving or loaning him the money he needs."

Shelley got up and walked around the table to give Roy a big hug, and a kiss on the cheek. "The world needs more people like you," she said. Still draped on Roy's neck, she smiled and winked at Pete. "You don't want to lend him money for a truck to move his things, so you are sending him home. In a truck!"

Roy turned his head to smile at her. Shelley beamed back at him. "Trust you to make that connection. Yes, we could do that. The schedule will be too tight this week, but if we gave him a week to organize, I could spare the truck and a couple of extra men to move him the following week."

"This gal is good at getting her way," he said to Pete.

"Yes, I have noticed that on the odd occasion," Pete laughed.

"So I will have a couple of days to try to get as much information as possible from Rafael, before he goes back. You're going to be cavorting off to Tucson anyway," Shelley said.

"Yes. But I should have some lab results by Wednesday night. Maybe you could come down for a day or two so we can discuss stuff."

Shelley noted her Dad was trying to suppress a little grin. "I guess I could spare her for a couple of days," he said. "I'm sure you 'will' need to discuss 'stuff'."

"Great!" Pete grabbed a piece of paper and a pen. "This is the address and phone for my humble digs in Tucson — not that I will be there very much. Most of the time I'll be at the university. And I'll have my cell phone off most of the time, because I'm just about out of minutes for the month. I seem to have mysteriously chewed up a lot more cell time recently — specifically in the last week!"

"Some people like to talk a bit," Roy laughed. "What about your job at Chemulous?"

"I already sent them an email — resigning effective immediately. So I am now officially unemployed, which is going to bite."

"Hmmm," Roy mused. "Let's talk when you're back. Tomorrow I'll make a couple of calls, and see if we can initiate some action on your former employer. If we have reasonable suspicion they are trafficking undocumented workers, that should be enough to get law enforcement involved. If they are raided for that, it will be easier to collect evidence of their other schemes. Right now I'm ready to turn in."

"And I have to get back to my room, get cleaned up, packed, and ready for the road tomorrow," Pete replied, so I need to get moving myself.

And only a half hour of cuddling later, he was actually back in his truck and headed home. Shelley planned to come down to his place in Tucson on Wednesday night after work, arriving sometime around nine. She would come back home on the weekend. He would have to settle for that.

On Monday Shelley went about her work in a bit of a daze. She wanted to search out more information on the net about weather modification, and who was advocating what; she wanted to talk more with Rafael, and hoped he would allow her to tape the information; and mostly she just wanted to be where Pete was. This was a very new emotion for her, and was taking some time to get used to!

Pete had phoned from the house where he was boarding for the summer to let Shelley know he was on his way, and to be double sure she had the address and phone number for his place in Tucson. Wednesday night seemed a long way off to both of them.

Early on Tuesday, Roy contacted a friend who worked for the FBI and was stationed in the field office in Phoenix, just to check on jurisdictional issues — without providing too much detail. He wanted Rafael south of the border first.

He did, however, alert Jack to the potential that Chemulous trucks might be trafficking immigrants into the U.S., with an understanding that a larger conspiracy might be involved. That would give the authorities time to increase surveillance, and hopefully catch Chemulous in the act. Roy also called a former classmate who was now a senior Senator for California.

"Well Roy, there have been numerous reports and conspiracy theories over the past few years. The official government position is that there is nothing going on. Of course we have both been around long enough to know that where there is a lot of smoke, especially smoke from certain government departments, there is often a fire.

"But all of our attempts to get a proper Senate or Congressional inquiry have been stymied thus far. If what you have told me can be independently verified, we might push a full inquiry through this time. But we would need good bipartisan support.

"The two angles that would get the most traction in Arizona would be the 'illegals', which always seems to get their dander up, and the threat to the ground water and agriculture — if this stuff is as toxic as you say it is."

They had discussed the politicians most likely to support a request for an inquiry, and Roy added that to his to-do list for the week.

At supper, he filled Shelley in on the details of his two conversations. He also mentioned that one of the workers with whom Rafael was staying had managed to get a message to Rafael's wife, leaving out the details, but letting her know that her husband was okay, would be back on Wednesday, and to start preparing to move out of the village by the following week.

"Have you talked to Pete again?" he asked.

"No. I tried to call his place, but there was no answer, and would you believe he doesn't have voice mail? ... In this age?"

"Well, maybe he doesn't have that many girls trying to get a hold of him, or at least not ones who chew up his whole month's cell phone allowance in a week".

"He expected to be at the university really late for a couple of nights, so that is probably where he is," she replied.
"So you don't figure he is out with another girl?" he teased. He regretted saying it as soon as it passed his lips.

Shelley's face clouded over in a way he had not seen since Jane left. Jane's betrayal of them both still left a scar. "Oh Dad!" was all she said.

"I'm sorry Shelley Girl," he apologized. "You know I was just kidding."

"Yes, I know," she replied unconvincingly. "But I haven't known him that long. ... Anyway, I have to get going. I told Rafael I would come over after supper and record everything he can tell me about Chemulous and his village."
....

They had chatted around the small table in Rafael's room for nearly three hours. Shelley looked up from her notes. Rafael looked pensive.

"Is something wrong?"

"I just theeking that big truck trailer, not good for Esmeralda and kids. No safe locked in back with furniture and theengs."

"Surely there's another way for your wife and family to get to Los Algodones?"

"Oh yes, my wife, she drive my car. I not talking wife," he laughed. "Esmeralda our goat! Has two kids."

"Oh! Well yes, that would be a problem. Maybe... Would they be able to travel in Pete's truck?"

"Eef I make chicken wire cage, so they don't try jump out, might work. You and Pete do that for me? You do so much a'ready."

"I think we could arrange it. I'll talk to him by phone or when I see him tomorrow night, and let you know. I am sure he will be okay with doing that."

Shelley looked again at her notes, and then at the clock on the wall. "I really need to be going. I'm glad we were able to talk. Thank you. I understand a lot more of what is going on now. Take care of that leg, and I hope you have a safe trip home tomorrow."

It was nearly eleven o'clock when Shelley got home. She had a lot of information recorded, but it had taken more time than she expected and Pete had called when she was away. Roy left a note by the phone with the number. Shelley was dead tired and still a bit out of sorts. She looked at the time, wondering if she should call or just crash. Finally, she picked up the phone and dialed the number.

Pete answered on the third ring. "Hi M'Lady. Thought you must have already settled in for your beauty sleep."

"No. I only just got in. I had a long chat with Rafael after supper. He told me a few new things..."

"Drat. Call waiting. My mom, from L.A. Can I call you right back?"

"Don't bother. I'll see you tomorrow anyway. Goodnight."

As tired as she was, Shelley tossed and turned for what seemed like hours before finally drifting into a troubled sleep. She woke late, to find yet another note by the phone. Pete was just on his way out, and was expecting her about nine that evening. Time seemed to crawl all morning.

When she met Roy at lunch, he updated her on Rafael — who was now safely on the Mexican side of the border — and on the Chemulous situation. Seems that one of their trucks was surreptitiously photographed at the border crossing, and it looked like another stowaway was on board. His FBI friend had put a tail on the truck, so they would find out if it delivered the worker to the local Chemulous plant.

"If they can make a case that Chemulous is knowingly bringing people in, then they can get the authorization for a raid," he explained. "They can then seize any records, including Pete's analysis results, shipping and billing records, the works. So Pete's non-disclosure document becomes a non-issue. If there is enough evidence to build a criminal case, that will give the politicians what they need to spread the net wider, and demand a full Senate probe".

"That's great Dad," she replied. "Can I tell Pete when I see him?"

"Better to keep it quiet for now. I, or I should say 'we', already know much more than we should. If Pete should get called in for questioning, it would be best if he knew nothing about this FBI operation.

"Speaking of Pete, why don't you head out after lunch? There's nothing critical waiting on you, and that way you won't have to drive in the dark."

She did not need much convincing. By two, her red Fiesta was speeding toward Tucson. As she entered the outskirts, the rush hour traffic was building. Pete had expected to finish his work by late afternoon today, so she pulled into a shopping center and dialed his home, on the off chance he would be back already.

"Yes?" a female voice answered.

Chapter 11 — Surprise

Totally caught off guard, Shelley blurted out, "Oh, I was expecting Pete."

"He's not home yet, but should be here shortly. Can I tell him who called?"

Shelley took a deep breath. "No, I, ... I can call him later."

She took some time to compose herself. Then she turned back onto the road and continued toward her destination, not knowing what to expect — or how to act.

"Maybe just a casual friend or house keeper," she thought to herself. But that didn't make much sense, and she knew it! Pete wasn't expecting her until nine, so why was another woman 'expecting' him home?

Pete's small house was on a quiet street in an older part of the city. Shelley drove by slowly, checking the addresses. Yes. That was the house alright, and a woman was squatting with her back to the road, cleaning the dead vegetation from the desert plants in the front yard. She had long hair over her shoulders, and was dressed for the afternoon heat in a colorful blouse and short shorts. *"Nice butt,"* Shelley thought angrily.

She continued around the corner and parked on a side street. As she walked slowly back, she saw Pete's old truck approach from the other end of the street. Leaning in the shade against the base of a palm tree, she watched him stop the truck, jump out, and run to hug this floozy.

She felt her world crumble. As the two distant figures headed for the house with their arms around each other's waists, Shelley spun on her heels and headed back to the car, flicking off her cell phone as she went.

She arrived back home shortly before nine. Roy met her at the door, a look of concern on his face. He could tell she had been crying.

"What happened?," he asked.

"Give me some space, Dad. I'm not ready to talk about it. Maybe tomorrow."

After almost six hours of driving, amid huge emotional turmoil, Shelley was exhausted. As she headed for her room, she stopped and turned to face him. "And if Pete calls, I have no interest in talking to him!" She went into her room and closed the door.

Shortly after nine the phone rang. Roy answered. "Yes I do. She's okay. She's here at home — just got in a few minutes ago. ... No. I don't know what happened. I thought you might know. ... She's already gone to bed. Maybe in the morning. ... Yes, I'm sure you are. Goodnight."

She was not up by the time Roy headed to work. Shortly after nine she heard the phone ring. After five rings the answering machine kicked in. It was almost certainly "two-timing" Pete. Shelley pondered what to do. She was booked off for the next two days.

As she ate breakfast, she looked out at the surrounding desert, and the mountains in the distance. Then she got up, rinsed up her dishes, and went back to her room. She packed up her camera gear, pup tent, and outdoor clothes. The phone rang a second time. She finished her packing, and returned to the kitchen to pick up some food. She checked the messages. Both were from Pete, asking her to call, and leaving his home, his cell, and another number. He sounded quite upset. She deleted the messages.

"You made your bed — go lie in it," she thought. After scribbling a quick note to Roy, she headed for the car. There was another local area that she wanted to explore as part of her research. A couple of days in the wilderness would clear her head.

R.A. Abell

Chapter 12 — Rhona

By Friday afternoon Shelley was ready to head home. The new trails she had explored were interesting, and she did find some additional examples for her study, but somehow the trip did not have the usual lightening effect on her soul that she had always experienced in the past on this type of excursion.

It didn't help that every time she flicked on her phone to check in with Roy, there was yet another message from Pete, which she immediately deleted. *"How long is it going to take before he gets the message,"* she wondered.

On the way down the trail, she came across another pair of towhees. Seemed she just couldn't avoid reminders. She wondered how long these blues would last. She had not experienced this kind of sadness since her mom left over twelve years ago. It had taken months, and the move from California to this beautiful desert, to finally pull her out of her funk. She had vowed at the time to never make herself that vulnerable again.

By a quarter past five she was driving into their yard. A strange car was parked on the side of the driveway. It was unusual for Roy to have business acquaintances to the house. As she went in the front door, she heard Roy talking to someone out on the patio.

She looked at her dusty clothes and decided to hit the shower before joining them.

Fifteen minutes later she finished dressing, brushed out her hair, and headed for the back patio. She could smell the barbecue, and noticed a wine bottle on the kitchen table.

As she headed out the door, she stopped abruptly in mid stride. Roy's guest was female, and she recognized that butt in short shorts immediately! *"What in hell is she doing here?"*

Before she could retreat, Roy spotted her.

"Shelley Girl! Glad you're back. Come over and meet Rhona."

The woman turned to face her, and Shelley got another shock. She was very attractive, fit, tanned, and somewhere in her late forties or early fifties!

The woman took a couple of quick strides towards her, put one hand on each shoulder in a familiar relaxed way, and looked her over from top to bottom.

Then she looked Shelley directly in the eye. "You're drop dead gorgeous, and I think you 'broke' my son." Shelley didn't know if she should laugh or cry.

"You're Pete's mom," Shelley burst out, and here I thought...."

"You thought I was the competition," Rhona replied. "It was two long days of Pete's moping before I finally figured out what must have happened, and got some answers out of him. You called just before five on Wednesday, didn't you?" Shelley nodded.

"I noticed the little red car go by a short time later. You were driving slowly, like you were looking for something. I knew Pete was expecting you, because he told me on the phone when I called Tuesday night, to let him know about my surprise trip. I knew then that something was up because he never ever bothered me about his casual dates.

But he said you weren't coming till around nine. Not wanting to be a nuisance, I had checked into a motel a few blocks away. It was noon today before I got anything out of him. I haven't seen him that down about anything or anyone since his dad died.

"So you saw me in the yard, and then saw him arrive home, and give his old mother a big hug, right?" she continued, "... and came to the wrong conclusion."

Shelley's eyes teared up. "Oh I'm so sorry. How could I be so stupid! ... So suspicious!"

Rhona pulled her into an embrace. "Let me assure you that Pete is faithful like a puppy dog. And he is head over heels for you, so I'm sure it's fixable."

"I can see the confusion," Roy chipped in. "Rhona could easily pass for half her age. ... You joining us for supper?"

Rhona smiled at him over her shoulder. Turning back to Shelley, Rhona jerked a thumb in Roy's direction and half whispered: "He's cute. Can he cook?"

Shelley grinned. "He can, and he's faithful like a puppy dog too. ... Where is Pete now?"

"He drove his truck back from Tucson. Said he was going up to his 'thoughtful spot' to figure stuff out. He didn't know I was coming here. He said something about a small cave."

Shelley turned to her Dad. "I'll pass on supper, Dad. I have some 'crow' to eat. You two have fun. I think you have a lot in common." As she turned to go, she smiled warmly at Rhona. "I don't expect to be back tonight, maybe not until Sunday, so you're welcome to use my room if you want to stay over."

"That's kind of you, Shelley. I might take you up on that." Roy's eyebrows rose, and he looked at Shelley quizzically. She grinned back at him, giggled, and skipped and bounced back into the house.

She came back out moments later in her leather skirt and a frilly blouse. Roy and Rhona were sitting side by side, and just raising their glasses in a toast. Shelley waved. "See you both tomorrow — or more likely Sunday. I'll give you a call."

She found his truck parked in the expected spot. The sun was already low, and the shadows lengthening. It was getting quite dark as she entered the wash. As she moved closer, she could see him on the ledge, hunkered over his fire, staring into the flames. The crackle of the fire masked her approach in the gathering gloom. She started up the steep slope. As she neared the ledge, he got up and moved to the end.

"Hey, careful where you aim that Lancelot!"

There was a stunned silence above.

"Finish your business, and then give me a hand up. I'm getting hypothermia down here. I hope you have a cure."

She could hear the deep smile and relief in his voice. "Yes M'lady. With the greatest of pleasure."

...

They sat side-by-side staring into the fire, Pete's sleeping bag round their shoulders. It had taken a long while to get through the whole story. Shelley alternately laughed and cried over her stupidity, and her compounding of the problem by refusing to answer his calls.

"I feel just horrible to have doubted you, when you have always been the perfect gentleman. I guess maybe I doubted myself a bit too. Maybe I'm not fully over my mother's betrayal, and some of the insecurity that it caused."

Pete was incredulous to think she could have mistaken his mother for a much younger woman. "I was born when she was in her early twenties, but she will be fifty soon. Difficult to imagine her being mistaken for a young floozy!"

"Well, when I saw her poking about in the plants, all I really got a good look at was her long legs and very nice butt, and you have to admit that you seem to have some attachment to that particular part of the feminine anatomy," she grinned.

"Guilty as charged on that one," he admitted, giving her bum a playful pinch. "Though there are lots of other interesting parts too."

"She's damn sexy for her age," Shelley went on. "Wait till you see how Roy looks at her," she added, laughing.

"Seriously though, making the mistake was bad enough. But refusing to call you back, and ignoring you calls was unconscionable. I can't tell you how sorry I am for that. It is not the way to ever treat someone you love." She stared solemnly into the fire.

"You're right about that," he said, taking her chin gently in his hand and turning her head to look into her face, "but that big 'L' word works both ways. It also means genuine acceptance and forgiveness, and since I fully plan on spending the rest of my life with you, you already have that, M'Lady."

She searched his eyes in the waning light of the fire. "I think I need that hypothermia cure Lancelot."

Chapter 13 — New Trails

On the way down from the ledge on Sunday morning, they took some time to discuss the Chemulous situation. Pete's prof had independently verified and recorded the toxic ingredients on Shelley's filter.

They had also run Internet searches, and found a couple of technical publications — suggesting these combinations would be particularly effective in reducing the solar flux at the surface.

Both were written by the same researcher — who appeared to have moved from one small obscure university to another over a period of ten years. None of his papers had made it into peer-reviewed journals.

"My prof was not impressed with his logic, or the strength of his references. I wonder if my mom could run down anything on his research funding," Pete mused. "Now, she mainly provides part-time logistics support for a senator and a couple of California congressmen, but she used to do forensic accounting."

...

Roy and Rhona were just sitting down for lunch when Shelley's car and Pete's old truck rattled into the yard. Shelley noticed that Rhona was wearing a fairly revealing and figure flattering sundress, and they both conveyed a relaxed comfort around each other.

They were so engrossed in their conversation that they waved to the kids only briefly, before returning to their discussion.

Shelley popped over to kiss Pete solidly as he got out of his truck. She jerked a thumb in the parents' direction, and giggled. Pete headed over to greet them, while Shelley took her things into the house.

She giggled again when she found her bed exactly as she had left it on Friday night. Things were progressing rather quickly — and why not? They were two very attractive and competent people, with only their kids in their lives. They still had a lot of good years ahead of them.

When Shelley joined the others, Rhona got up from her chair to give her a big hug. "Well he was broken, but you seem to have fixed him. And just for once, I think he's happy his mother interfered".

Pete nodded his agreement.

"So, am I — for a couple of reasons," Roy chipped in.

"Uh huh," she replied, flashing him a big smile. She reached over and gave his hand a squeeze as she sat down again. "Sit down you two. I made enough for everyone, thinking you might be back soon."

They were just finishing up dessert when two official-looking cars rolled into the yard — the first with a big FBI logo on the door, the other unmarked. Roy excused himself, and went to meet them, while Rhona quickly cleared the dessert dishes and took them into the house.

A large man emerged from the lead car and shook Roy's hand vigorously. They spoke quietly for a few moments, and then came over to the patio.

"Jack, this is my daughter Shelley, and her friend Pete. Jack is an FBI field officer in the Phoenix office. I've known him for years. Seems they raided the Chemulous plant early this morning, and got quite a haul. Jack, Pete worked there for a couple of months as a summer student running the spectrometer, so he might be able to help you out in interpreting what went on there."

They were sitting down at the patio table when Rhona came out with a fresh pot of coffee and extra cups. She stopped abruptly when she saw the guest.

"Jack, I didn't expect to see you here, of all places!"

She put the tray down as he rose to meet her, and they engaged in a warm hug. Roy's eyes narrowed. "You two know each other?"

"Worked together on a slew of projects over the years. One of the best damn forensic accountants I ever met. She and my wife Marci became great friends, but we haven't seen each other since Marci and I moved to Arizona," Jack replied.

Shelley hid her grin as she watched her dad visibly relax.

"How long are you in the area, Rhona?" Jack asked?

"I'm not sure. I originally figured about a week. I was making some inquiries for the Senator, and that also gave me an opportunity to spend some time with Pete. But some other stuff has come up," she replied, casting a quick glance at Roy.

"Good night! Pretty shabby of a Federal agent not to make the connection. Last time I saw Pete I think he was about four!"

"They do grow up fast it seems."

"Yes, they do. ... I'll have to double check with my superiors in Washington, but since he's one of the 'good guys' in this caper, I don't think it will be a problem that he is related to you," he mused.

"Problem?" she asked.

"Well, since you are one of the best in the business, and are still on our suppliers list, I was thinking you might want to help out with this one. The agents who took an initial look at the books and computer records have already uncovered at least five numbered companies in the transactions. From past experience, I am guessing that is the tip of the iceberg. ... You would probably need to stay in the area for a few months though. Any interest?"

She glanced at Roy, who was clearly delighted with the idea. "I might be interested. Better clear it upstairs before we get too excited."

After Jack left, Pete and Shelley filled their parents in on the things they had found out so far. When the topic turned to the 'positive research findings' of an otherwise obscure university professor, Rhona broke in.

"Not that surprising in today's academia," she said, "with its emphasis on external funding. Scientific rigor is too often relegated to second place behind commercial interests of individuals or companies who are paying the bills. Studies that are not 'positive' to the sponsor never see the light of day. But questionable studies that appear to support a preferred direction, or to debunk a 'real' study unfavorable to the sponsor, easily make it to publication."

"Does that actually happen?" Roy asked. "When I was in university, it was all about scientific rigor. I can't imagine any of my profs would have sold out their science for a commercial interest."

"And I'm sure that many still have those ethics, but the whole scene has changed since you and I were there," she replied.

"Universities used to be primarily about learning, and were run by academics. Today they are run as businesses, by hard-nosed business types who are focused on cash flow and the bottom line. From the late seventies, universities started focusing on intellectual property and technology transfer. That gradually turned university research into a commodity, which is sold — and frequently bought in advance."

"So you think this prof is coming up with these theories to justify a line of research that allows Chemulous to dispose of toxic waste, and he is being funded to publish papers that support them?"

"We've seen things like that before, in other cases that I worked on," she replied. "Finding the links is just a case of 'follow the money'."

"You would think people would get wise to that kind of thing, and that with only one source of information, it would not get any attention," Shelley observed, "but I guess it also depends on mainstream media."

"Look at the whole climate change denial," Pete chimed in. "Nearly all of the 'denial science' was traced back to a single lab that was heavily funded by oil interests. But many media outlets seemed to jump on it, and repeat the claims ad nauseam. Few readers of these rags would bother to trace the report back to the source."

"That's true," Shelley added, "but that doesn't seem to have happened here. It took a lot of digging for me to find out much of anything. Why the difference?"

There was silence around the table for a moment. Roy was the first to speak. "In the Chemulous case, there would be no need to 'convince' the public — just convince a single agency who can get the job done. The less the public knows, the better. Especially since the taxpayer is probably footing the bill!"

"I expect you're right about that," Rhona replied. "And if a government department is involved, that will slow things down. For all the 'freedom of information' and government 'transparency' we are supposed to have, that's not how it works in real life."

"But we're not going to solve the world's problems sitting around this table, and if I plan to take up Jack's offer — assuming he can get it approved — I need to give a heads-up to my current employers that I might not be back in California for a while."

"Roy, can I patch into your network from my tablet, so I can access my email?"

"Sure," he replied quickly. "If you are going to be staying here for some time, we might as well set you up properly. I'll go fire up the server. Be right back."

She raised her eyebrows, and gave him a quizzical look, as he headed for the house. When she looked back at Pete and Shelley, they were both grinning. "What?" she said defensively.

R.A. Abell

Chapter 14 — Girl Talk

Rhona looked at the two young people smiling back at her. After a moment of thought, she looked directly at Shelley and asked, "Could you and I have a girl chat? Pete, I know it will be difficult for you to spare her for a few minutes, but we do need to talk."

"I can probably last for up to fifteen minutes before withdrawal symptoms hit and I turn into a raving lunatic. As long as you are prepared to take that chance."

Shelley stood and detached her hand from his. "Knightly perseverance, Lancelot. Buck up."

He rose and bowed stiffly. "Yes M'lady. If you ask it of me, I must persevere."

She smiled brightly at him, and turned to Rhona. "You trained him well."

Rhona laughed. "If you say so. It doesn't always show this much! Let's take a stroll."

They walked through the yard and down to the fenced pasture. Shelley was quick to point out every plant, and extol the virtues of their place and their life here, as she bounced and skipped in typical Shelley fashion.

Rhona observed her with a mixture of amusement and admiration, before leaning back against the fence and taking a moment to just soak up the ambiance of the day. "We do need to talk about some stuff," she said finally.

Shelley came to lean against the fence beside her, half turning to face her. "Okay, that would be nice. Since my mom and dad divorced when I was thirteen, I haven't had a 'mom' to share with."

"That must have been very difficult for you."

"It was, but it was harder for Roy. He had to cope with his own loss as well as mine. I sometimes marvel that we pulled through it. But he is pretty special."

"Yes, I have discovered that. I met him only two days ago, and I feel like I know him already — like I have known him for years. And that's not typical for me. I don't think I've so much as held a man's hand for maybe five years, let alone...," she trailed off, staring into the distance.

Shelley took Rhona's two hands in hers. "Let alone sleeping with him?" she grinned.

"I guess I should at least have messed your bed up a bit," Rhona replied with a wry smile. "I really wasn't planning or expecting it to go that far that fast. It scares me a little! We have both been through a lot, and it would be hard on us — and maybe on you and Pete — if it didn't work out. It might be safer if Roy and I just stayed friends."

"And it would have been safer for me to stay at home and watch television, rather than go gallivanting off in the desert by myself so I could meet that handsome, intelligent, and thoroughly goofy son of yours. I don't happen to think that kind of 'safe' is what life is about. Have you heard the song, 'Standing Outside the Fire'?"

"I have, ... and you're right. It isn't about 'merely surviving', is it?"

"No, it's not. As upset with things as I was on Friday, I couldn't help noticing the way you and dad interacted — at every level! When I suggested you stay over, I almost burst to see his momentary panic-pleasure attack. The panic part lasted about ten seconds — until you said yes."

"I didn't necessarily expect my bed would be required," she laughed. "And from what I saw this morning when we got back, I think your interaction at every level is working out just fine."

Rhona's eyes misted up, and she pulled Shelley into a huge hug. "It's sure easy to see why Pete is so smitten with you, Shelley Girl."

"And it's easy to see why he is who he is," Shelley replied.

"The double upside is that I wouldn't have to worry about my step-mom not getting along with my mother-in-law," she laughed, "or my step-brother not getting along with my husband! Keeps all that stuff really simple."

"Has Pete actually discussed marriage?"

"Not yet, and I am sure the same is true for Roy with you. Of course in your case, it has been only two days! Pete and I have had a whole week!

"But working together, I'm sure we can fix both those problems in short order. Pete said he would be getting the 'don't screw up and lose her' lecture from you, so it would just be a simple variant. Besides, if they know for sure the answer is yes before they pop the question, it's much easier for them," she said conspiratorially. "Then we could have a double wedding! How awesome would that be!"

Rhona pushed Shelley to arms length, studied her face for a moment, and then returned to the hug.

"No 'merely surviving'," she mused quietly. Then she replied brightly. "Yes, my daughter, I think together we can pull that off! Till then, we live in 'sin'!" she giggled.

Roy and Pete watched the two girls come back up the yard. Part way back, they stopped while Shelley demonstrated skipping. After a couple of tries, Rhona synced in, and they covered the last fifty feet with their arms around each others' waists skipping in more or less perfect coordination.

They arrived giggling, and a spot out of breath. "Roy, this girl's spirit is infectious! It is going to be very good for me to be around her for the next while. She makes me realize I am way too serious a lot of the time."

She came around the table, leaned over, and kissed him full on the lips. "You did a marvelous job of raising her. I'm impressed. ... Now I do need to get those emails off. Did you get me set up on the network?"

Roy blushed a little, glancing at Shelley and Pete to see their reaction to this outward show of affection. Seeing that they were totally okay with it, and busy with their own banter, he relaxed a bit.

"Well, the server is up. We'll need your tablet for the next step."

"Okay. It's in my bag in our room. I'll go get it. It will be nice to not be living out of a suitcase for awhile."

It took a minute for the implications of her simple statement to hit him. He looked at Shelley. "So why are you looking like the cat that swallowed the canary?"

"Oh, nothing in particular and everything in general," she giggled, giving Pete's hand a squeeze.
...

The rest of the day seemed to pass quickly. Roy and Rhona worked through their respective emails, and then spent an hour or two relaxing around the patio table in the hottest part of the day.

Shelley finally was getting around to sorting through the hundreds of pictures she had taken since she had started up that trail just over a week ago.

Pete was sitting cross-legged on her four-poster bed, reading through some of Roy's engineering books on Solar Energy. Shelley looked up at his studious expression, as he concentrated all of his attention on his reading.

She wasn't used to this serious side, not that it would take her much effort if she decided to 'distract' him. *"Not yet,"* she grinned to herself. *"Later"*. Now she was distracted! *"Focus,"* she thought. *"Since I'm keeping this one, we have all the time in the world."* She hummed a bit of the Louis Armstrong classic as she went back to her sorting.

"Shelley. Do you have something I can make some notes on?" he asked a few minutes later.

She opened her desk drawer, found an unused coil notebook and pen, and took them to him where he sat, giving him a little peck on the forehead as she did so.

"You seem very engrossed in those books," she commented.

"Well I do need to get up to speed quickly, if I am to make myself useful."

She looked at him quizzically.

"Oh. ... You know with all the conversation turns after you and mom got back from your girl talk, I think I totally forgot to tell you about our guy talk. Roy offered me a job. Naturally I didn't want to make any hasty decisions, so I thought hard about it, ... for about five seconds!"

Shelley threw her arms around his neck. "Pete, that's wonderful!"

He suddenly grabbed her arms, tipped her backwards on the bed, and kissed her — books spilling from his lap. After a short time, he propped himself up just a bit, still holding her arms down, and smiled.

"Mind you, it is going to be challenging work. Some of Roy's staff can be distracting. One of them is delightfully distracting! Keeping her in line on the job site will be difficult. Now back to work!

"See," he said in mock indignation, returning to his previous seated position, "you made me lose my place. No time for hanky panky — not yet!"

Shelley bounced up from the bed, muttering under her breath about another slave driver. She spun round when she reached her chair. "You have no idea how delighted I am, Lancelot, or maybe you do!"

"Knights feel delight too, M'Lady, now back to your needle point!"

A few minutes later he heard her printer start up. She got up from her desk, and rattled around in her closet, coming out with a new frame. After a time she came over to the bed, removed the picture that hung on the rear wall, and put it in a lower drawer. She handed Pete the replacement.

"I think this is a better choice for our room, don't you?"

Pete looked at the smiling photo of Roy and Rhona huddled close at the picnic table, clinking their wine glasses together, foreheads almost touching.

"Got to love a long telephoto lens," she laughed. "They had no idea they were on candid camera."

Pete looked at it thoughtfully, and then turned to hang it on the hook just recently occupied by the serious-faced woman he assumed was her birth-mom.

"Yes, I agree. This really is more appropriate for our room. But do you think Roy is ready to see my face at the breakfast table?"

"Considering his obvious interest in seeing your mom at the breakfast table, and her unabashed enthusiasm for accommodating that, I somehow don't think he will raise serious objections," she laughed. "But you will have to help with the wash! ... Can you get out of the deal at that run-down place you are staying in?"

"Not a problem. When I told the landlady I quit my job at Chemulous, she wanted to know how soon I could move out. Said she had a couple of girls needing a place. I think they are friends of the two 'working girls' down the hall!" he replied.

She looked at him funny.

"Hey, no worries. I might be a Knight, but I'm not Don Quixote," he laughed. "You could come with me while I get my stuff. It wouldn't take long. All I have is clothes, a few books, my laptop, razor and toothbrush. Let me finish this chapter, and then we can fire up my steed and go make the big move."

"Okay," she said. "I just need to finish sorting a few more of these. I'm working from latest to earliest. ... Think your mom would like to put your artwork up on the fridge, Michael Angelo?" she said, bursting into giggles.

"Hey, he made a pretty good living with his art," he said in · mock seriousness.

"I'd stick with your day job," she laughed.

"Well Roy seemed pretty impressed with some of my concept drawings, but then working on a drafting table with proper tools is a spot easier than fire charcoal on a rock medium — especially when the audience is expected to arrive for the art show at any second. ... Maybe the earlier version is more suited to the fridge. With great art, copies don't cut it anyway" he intoned.

Shelley laughed, and went back to her work. She found the towhee photos, and selected the best to show the plumage or the behavior. Only another twenty shots to go.

"Pete, get over here and look at these images! I'm almost certain this is where that toxic mist came from. I fluked a better shot of that plane than I thought!"

R.A. Abell

Chapter 15 — Up the Ante

Pete came over to stare at the blown up photo on Shelley's large-screen monitors. The large plane could be seen clearly, vapor trails streaming back from the wings.
"I got several shots, but this is the best one I have of the plane."

"Certainly good enough to identify the type," Pete replied. "And another interesting thing! There are more vapor trails than there are engines! It looks like a military aircraft, but I'm not the expert on that. Mom's political contacts can get to the sources. Among other things, they have worked with veterans groups on the Agent Orange fiasco. ... But what is this funny blur here?"

"That's a humming bird. My auto focus happened to synch in on the plane in this shot. I had the aperture wide open, which caused the bird and the ocotillo to blur out. I was dialing in settings like mad trying for the perfect shot. That was the best of the plane, but here is the prize winner!"

The photo was striking! On the left half of the image, high on the top of the stem, a tiny humming bird hovered motionless, his long beak deep in the red blossom, his wings a blur of motion. To the right, the blue sky was split by the white trails of vapor, the aircraft clearly visible on the leading edge.

"Besides being a movie-star-tomboy-with-an-attitude, you are one damn fine photographer. That one should be a winner! But it also will be valuable in making the case."

"How so Sherlock?"

"Elementary my dear Watson! Once we know what kind of aircraft that is, we know its size. We also know the size of the hummingbird. So it is a simple matter of geometry to get a reasonable estimate of how high the aircraft is flying. You did say he seemed very low to be generating a contrail?"

"You will make a fine engineer, at least when you don't allow yourself to be distracted," she said, half-heartedly pushing his exploring hand away, before deciding to get a spot distracted herself.

"Okay. Enough already. Later, not yet! Back to the books Lancelot, and let me get these filed properly before I accidentally hit the delete key while fending you off!"
...

Shelley turned her computer off. "Okay Lancelot, I'm finished here. Ready to go get your stuff? I'm sure going with you. Don't want those ladies of the night snagging you for a loyal pet."

"No danger of that M'Lady. Okay if I leave my books on your, ... I mean 'our' bed?"

"Depends. You planning on reading engineering books tonight, while I drift quietly off to la-la land? ... I thought not!" she laughed, looking at his wide-eyed expression.

"So in the interest of not wasting time later, when you could be waiting on me hand and foot — and other places — why don't I clear these teddy bears off this shelf now, and give you a spot for your stuff?"

As they left the house, Shelley noticed Roy and Rhona huddling, or maybe cuddling, on the grassy bank at the edge of the patio.

"I'll meet you at the truck. Just want to let Dad know where we're going." Roy looked up as she bounced over.

"Hi Dad and Mom, sorry to interrupt."

Greeted with Roy's *"What con are you up to now?"* face, she continued innocently.

"Well she is already Pete's mother. You don't mind me calling you Mom, do you Rhona?"

Rhona silently mouthed *"You're good!"* before responding with a big smile. "Of course not, my lovely daughter. ... So, where are you two off to now?"

Shelley could see the struggle, but clearly Rhona's laughter suppression system worked better than her own.

"We're just driving into town to pick up Pete's things from that den of iniquity where he's been staying. Need anything from the store while we're in town, Dad?"

"Well, uh, no. I guess we can make some space in the office for the inflatable bed," he said uneasily.

"Why ever would you think that necessary?" Shelley asked.

"Perhaps your father thinks that people who are not married should not share a bed," Rhona chipped in helpfully.

Roy looked helplessly from one to the other. Shelley was the first one to flinch, starting with snorts and giggles that soon became gales of laughter. Rhona held out a spot longer, but not much.

"I get the distinct impression that I have just been out-maneuvered on my home turf," he said finally.

"Yep, you have, Napoleon, so you might as well surrender to the superior forces arrayed against you," Rhona replied, before capturing him between one arm and a pair of lips, while waving goodbye to Shelley with the free arm.

As she skipped up to the truck, Pete looked at her quizzically. "What was that all about?" he asked.
"Oh, nothing," she replied. "Just confirming the sleeping arrangements. No worries. It's all good."

Chapter 16 — New Beginning

Monday was a new beginning. As Pete quietly opened the bedroom door and stepped into the hallway, he almost ran into Roy.

Feeling somewhat sheepish, he mumbled an apology. He wasn't clear even in his own mind if it was because of the near collision, or because Roy's daughter was in the bed he had just left, sprawled in naked and peaceful slumber.

Roy looked at him for a moment, before clasping him round the shoulder. "Morning Son. Ready for some coffee? ... These women of ours expect us to wait on them, right? And I suspect we are both in way too deep to get out of their clutches."

"You're undoubtedly right about that, Dad. Even if we wanted to."

"Which I certainly don't," Roy replied. "Rhona is the best thing that has come into my life since Shelley was born. You think you are your own person, totally self sufficient, and then the balloon pops and you realize you are only a half a person until someone supplies that other half. And if it had not been for you, I wouldn't have either of them. So I owe you big time. That means I make the coffee ... today, anyway!"

Pete laughed. "I'm glad you two have hit it off so well. Since my Dad died, it has been hard on her. I haven't seen her so radiant in a long while."

...

As he slipped back into their room a few minutes later, a fresh coffee in his hand, Shelley opened her eyes and smiled that brilliant Shelley smile at him.

"Ah, my most beautiful Mistress Shelley is awake! Your faithful Jeeves has brought a morning libation. Do take care not to spill it on those beautiful distractions. It is much too hot for thy beautifully unclothed form."

Shelley laughed, taking the cup from him carefully and sipping from the edge.

"This beautifully unclothed form needs to get into a house coat and hit the shower chop chop. Today is a workday — and for you too Lancelot. And no goofing off on company time!"

...

It was mid-morning when Jack called. Rhona and Roy had cleared the dishes before Roy headed out to the job site. Rhona stayed behind to wash up some of her things, as she had not planned on being away for this long, and most of the clothes she had brought from L.A. were still at Pete's place in Tucson. When she finished her chat with Jack, she moved her wash to the drier and then called Roy at work.

"Hi. Thought you'd like to know that Jack called. ... Yes. He will have the contract ready for signing by tomorrow. He's sending a draft just after lunch. ... No. I could go into Phoenix to sign it tomorrow. He offered me office space there."

She smiled to herself as Roy went through all of the reasons she would not want to stay in Phoenix, followed by all of the reasons she could get more done if she stayed where she was.

"So it's all about my being more efficient," she teased. She had to cover the mouthpiece to avoid giving the game away too soon. "You would? I see. ... Well, I'm glad to know you feel that way. ... It would have been quite embarrassing to call Jack back and tell him I would take the space in Phoenix after all!

"Yes, I could have told you that in the beginning, but it was more fun this way. Besides, I like to have you tell me how much you want me around! ... No, I wasn't worried about raising your blood pressure. You're in great shape, and you know it. If you're concerned about your blood pressure, we just might have to give up some other activities," she giggled. ... "No, I thought not. Think of it as interval training!

"... Yes, I could join you for lunch. Good thing Shelley had a couple of things that fit me. But I will have to get right back here to finish my wash, and to review that contract when it comes in. Then I am going to need to do some shopping to tide me through until I can get some more of my duds sent up."

Chapter 17 — The Mexican Connection

By Tuesday all of the contract details were ironed out. Jack suggested he could bring the contract down in the late afternoon, and perhaps arrange to look over Shelley's photos at that time.

He arrived just after four. While Rhona picked through the legalese of the contract, Roy and Pete talked "shop". Shelley fired up her computer and Jack joined her to review the pictures.

A short time later, Jack came back into the kitchen, holding a USB memory stick. "Great photos that girl takes... though I passed on your artwork," he joked with Pete. He then opened his briefcase and pulled out a pocket-sized hard drive and waved it at Rhona.

"So if all of that is in order, just sign your life away on the dotted line and I give you two terabytes of Chemulous inside information. Deal?"

"I see here that the FBI will provide 24/7 protective surveillance if we request it," she commented.

Roy looked at Rhona with concern. "Do you think that might be necessary?" he asked.

"It would just be precautionary," Jack replied, "but these are not particularly nice people we are dealing with, and it doesn't make sense to take unnecessary chances. Probably not necessary at this point though, since there is not anything that would link our investigations to you.

"But there is one thing I need you to level on," he added, looking directly at Shelley and Roy. Who is 'Rafael', and where is he now?"

"Sorry Dad. 'Loose lips sink ships'. When we were going through my pictures, I guess I said something about 'Rafael'. climbing out of that truck."

Roy filled in the details. Jack made notes, asking only the occasional question. When Roy described the repatriation and Rafael's planned move to Los Algodones, Jack interjected.

"Okay, so he was not in good shape when you found him. You took care of him for three days, and then took him home. Now I could read you your Miranda rights before asking this, but I'm not going to. ... Did you ever ask Rafael about his papers or status?"

Roy looked nervously at each of the people around the table, before responding. "No, ... but ..."

Jack held up his hand. "No. Skip the 'but'. I didn't ask you about 'but'. So you specifically did not ask him about papers. You just took care of him, and then took him home? And you never offered him a job?"

Looking substantially relieved, Roy replied: "No, I did not offer him a job".

"Good. So you were not under legal obligation to ask for documentation, and you didn't. You just did the humanitarian thing, and took him south again. ... I can work with that. We're all on the same page here?"

Everyone nodded agreement.

"Rhona, since you are officially on the investigation now, you need to know this. It will all be in the public record anyway, but I would still ask that you keep this confidential.

"We tracked the employment history of Pete's supervisor back to New Mexico. He was one of the foremen in a company that was awarded a very large multi-year contract for hazardous waste cleanup at a former military test site there.

"It was a large site, and that work is still ongoing. In the proposal they submitted to win the bid, they referenced extensive landfill rehabilitation projects throughout Texas, mostly just community projects, but some fairly large ones.

"They operate an incinerator west of Pecos that is supposed to ultimately reduce everything to a glass-like slag that encapsulates the heavy metals pretty much like the rock they came from in the first place. So the proposal was to treat both streams, the military and the industrial-residential, in this same facility."

"That sounds massively energy intensive," Pete broke in.

"It is massively energy intensive, and on top of that, EPA requirements for emissions are stringent. But this company seems to have friends in high places.

"The plant was cited for violations once early on, but it seems that the inspector involved then took early retirement — and it looks like they were given a clean bill of health shortly after. The other interesting thing is that the energy use and slag tonnage is only a small fraction of what it should be for the volumes presumably going through!"

"So you figure they are just diverting it, and sending it across the border into Mexico?" Rhona asked.

"How could they get it across the border?" Shelley added.

"Change the dangerous goods signs, prepare a false manifest, and spread some money around. That would be all it would take," Jack replied. "Their cleanup projects pay very well — specifically because of the high energy costs — so if they can dodge those costs, then they make a fortune. If we can catch them shipping the stuff across the border with falsified labeling and documentation, we can shut them down. If we can prove conspiracy or bribery, then some folks might find themselves doing jail time."

"Then there is the whole issue on the other end of the pipeline," Rhona noted. Just at that point, her cell phone rang. "I'd better take this. It's the Senator."

The call was short. After she hung up, she turned to face the group. "Jack, you said they must have friends in high places? Sounds like you're right. The senator just found out that someone from the Senate Armed Services Committee is trying to get the investigation shut down!"

"Armed Services Committee!" Jack exclaimed. "That doesn't sound good. It's one of the most powerful committees in government. If they come down on the Chief, everything we have found out so far will go in a big box labeled 'forget'."

"The Senator thinks he can hold them off for a few days, maybe up to a week," Rhona replied, "but we'll have to move fast! He said to expect a call from the Mexican authorities about setting up a joint operation at the border.

"The Federales have also been tracking other events in Rafael's home town where Chemulous has the plant. There have been some nasty incidents in and around the town. The Mexican government is really interested in weeding out local officials who are getting rich by turning a blind eye to this kind of thing. And if the Mexican government gets involved with the Chemulous case, the Senator figures it will be a lot harder for anyone here to hush all of this up."

"We are on very good terms with our counterparts south of the border, so a joint operation could happen very quickly," Jack replied.

"Rhona, you are going to need some help getting through all that data. The contract specifically authorizes you to put extra bodies on this, as long as they have security clearance and are sworn to secrecy. As it happens, everybody in this room has already passed the background check. I had that done because you are all potential witnesses. Roy, do you have a fax here? I could get security clearance forms filled out and faxed for your signatures. Rhona would have to counter sign, as the contractor.

"I am, of course assuming everyone would be willing to pitch in? ... I rather thought so," he laughed at the enthusiastic response.

"Pete and I won't be around to sign tomorrow, though," Shelley replied.

"We have to go down and help Rafael move Esmeralda."

"His goat," Pete added.

Jack looked worried. "Is that wise? We don't know when things might come totally unglued down there. I can't directly protect you once you're south of the border."

"We should be fine," Pete replied. "We don't have to go directly through the town. Rafael lives a couple of miles to the south. We'll sign on the dotted line when we're back."

Chapter 18 — Moving Day

They crossed the border at Lukeville, headed south and then turned East. It would have been considerably shorter to cross at the nearest border point just north of Rafael's home town, but Pete did not want to chance running into the Chemulous trucks that traveled that route every day. Some of the drivers might recognize his pickup and start asking questions. The Chemulous plant was on the northeast side of town, while Rafael was in the south. By coming from the west, Pete figured they were less likely to be spotted.

As they neared the town, they could see the haze and smoke drifting south over the small valley. The air quickly took on the acrid smell of burning garbage.

Shelley wrinkled her nose. "Yeuch! Can you imagine having to breathe this air all the time, night and day?"

They soon found Rafael's small farm, located on a gently sloping hillside tucked into the left side of the valley. Just east of the road, the creek ran from the north, it's water looking greasy and gray. Roy's truck and crew had left for Mexico earlier than Pete and Shelley, and had taken a more direct route, so most of Rafael's belongings were already loaded. Pete parked on the side a ways down the narrow driveway, to leave room for the moving truck to get by.

Rafael hurried over to meet them, still hobbling with his sprained ankle. He took each of them into a typical Mexican embrace, thanking them yet again for helping him and his family to escape from the desolation and destruction that Chemulous had brought to their valley.

"So you are getting around better, " Pete observed, clapping Rafael on the shoulder.

"Si, zee town doctor wrap and make support. Says should be good another two weeks."

Shelley looked up the drive to the house, where Roy's men were just removing the ramp and shutting the trailer. Rafael's small tractor was loaded on an open trailer they would pull behind the main unit.

"Is your wife still here? I would love to meet her."

"No here Señorita, gone my sister's yesterday. You meet when we get Los Algodones."

"Just Esmeralda and kids," he grinned, remembering her confusion.

She laughed at his comeback. "So let's go meet Esmeralda!"

They stopped to briefly chat with Roy's crew, and ensure they had the necessary directions to Rafael's new farm. Pete helped them attach the small trailer on the rear hitch. Then, as the truck pulled out, they rounded behind the house toward an enclosed area, where Esmeralda and her two young held sway.

To the right, Shelley saw the carefully constructed wire cage that would keep the goats safely in Pete's truck. Ahead, at the back of the goats' enclosure, a field of new corn was already shoulder height and fully leaved, though not yet forming ears. Further back, the hillside was covered with dense shrub brush, unusually thick for such arid country.

Esmeralda kept herself positioned between the strangers and her two kids, but slowly sauntered closer to the fence, until after some minutes she allowed Shelley to scratch her ears.

Pete pulled out his pocket camera and took the picture, then repositioned himself for a second shot. As he moved to the other side, he noticed a movement on the road. A battered truck slowed and pulled into the drive. Two men were in the cab, and a third rode in the back — and he had what looked like a rifle!

Pete knew that gun laws in Mexico were much stricter than in the U.S., so it was very unusual to see them carried in the open. *"I have a bad feeling about this,"* he thought. He moved back to the fence beside Shelley and Rafael, where they were out of sight of the intruders, screened by Rafael's small house.

"There are three men in a truck out front, and it looks like they are armed! I think we would be wise to hide back in the trees."

Shelley could tell in an instant that this was not a Pete prank, even before the rattle of an assault rifle and the sound of breaking glass confirmed the danger. Esmeralda started, and raced for her shed, her kids bouncing behind.

Shelley moved to support Rafael's bad side, and they headed quickly up the fence line and into the small corn field. Fortunately the fence ran at an angle that kept the house between them and the gunmen, who seemed mainly focused on shooting up the house.

Rafael moved quickly in spite of his injury, and he and Shelley were in the field and partially screened by the corn foliage in a matter of seconds.

Pete brought up the rear, watching anxiously over his shoulder for any movement at the side of the house. Once within the cover of the corn, he ducked down and pulled out his cell to dial 066. An English speaking emergency operator was available, and with short bursts of gunfire clearly audible in the background, he had her attention immediately and was able relay the location.

By now Rafael and Shelley had reached the trees and were well concealed. Only at this point did Shelley realize that Pete was not with them. She watched in horror and disbelief as the window in the upstairs of the small house opened, and a single shot rang out.

In the field below, still focused on the near side of the house, Pete did not hear the gunshot. He did not even have time to register the pain, before everything went black.

Chapter 19 — Field of Fire

Rafael saw Pete go down, and had to hold Shelley back to keep her from running into the field.

"No do any good you run there, get shot too. If he dead, nothing we can do. If he wounded, we need get help. Neighbor Manuel just over hill. Come. Come quickly!"

Shelley shuddered and sobbed deeply, shaking her head from side to side. Then she turned, and taking Rafael's arm, started up the hill. As Rafael continued to favor his ankle, it was not clear who was supporting whom.

Single gunshots and bursts from automatic weapons continued to rattle behind them as they crossed the crest of the hill and started down toward the small house tucked into the trees. A plump woman standing on the porch shouted into the house, and then hurried up the path to meet them.

Shelley slumped against a tree, hardly conscious of her surroundings. Rafael and the señora spoke in rapid Spanish, as her husband came up the path to meet them. Rafael briefly introduced Josefina, and the woman reached out and held Shelley in her arms. Then, speaking gently in her own tongue, she helped Shelley the rest of the way down the path and into the house, while Manuel aided his friend.

Rafael noticed that the gunfire seemed to increase, and then after about five minutes, it abruptly stopped! Manuel hung up the phone, and he and Rafael consulted before Rafael turned to Shelley.

"Manuel's son, he in police. Police and Federales, they at my place. We go in Manuel's car. Better you stay here with Josefina."

Shelley stood abruptly. "No way," she said defiantly through her tears. "I have to know what happened to Pete, one way or the other. The police might not even know he is out there!"

...

It was a slow drive from Manuel's place, where the road wound down the hill to the west and south, finally meeting the main highway just before it turned north into the valley.

There, Shelley was surprised to see several federal police vehicles including trucks of heavily armed agents. She heard the telltale sound of one or more helicopters. As they drove north, they found a roadblock manned by the local police that prevented them from getting to Rafael's drive. Seeing their car approach, one of the officers came from behind the barricade.

"Mi hijo, José," Manuel exclaimed. Manuel and Rafael had a rapid fire exchange with Manuel's son. Rafael explained about Pete, indicating Shelley sitting dejectedly in the rear seat. José addressed Shelley in perfect English.

"I am sorry to hear of this señorita. I know only that two men on the property were killed and two others were wounded. I hope to hear that your Pete is one that survived. I believe the wounded were taken to the hospital in Puerto Peñasco. The air ambulance left just moments ago. If you will excuse me for a moment, I can see what my chief knows of this."

José walked back to his cruiser, and reaching through the window, brought his radio mic outside to place the call. It took some time before he seemed to connect to an information source on the other end. Shelley felt she could hardly breathe. Finally José returned to their car, looking somewhat puzzled.

"Señorita, it appears that one of the men taken to hospital was American, but according to our information he is an employee of Chemulous, as were the other three assailants. So he is under some suspicion. But he was found behind the house, did not appear to be armed, and we believe his cellphone was actually the source of the 066 call.

"Our information is that he suffered a head wound, but how serious we don't know. The Federal Police made the assault and handled the med-evac. We just provided backup. Since you are an American, you can decline, but the chief would like to talk with you to see if you can shed any light on what has happened here, if you would be willing."

Shelley did not know how to respond. She had not experienced policing outside of the U.S., and did not know what to expect. While she agonized about the best course of action, José reiterated the details in rapid-fire Spanish to Rafael and his father.

Rafael became quite agitated, and Shelley heard Pete's name and Esmeralda's used, with much gesturing. José listened gravely, then turned to Shelley.

"Señorita, I think we do not have a problem here, but it would nonetheless help if you could talk with the chief. He has been under some heavy political pressure, as there are some supporters of the chemical plant in the local government. But with the Federal Police now involved, we might see an end to this activity.

"If you can help the chief to connect the dots — I think that is the expression, no? — I can perhaps talk him into allowing me to escort you to Puerto Peñasco to see your friend. I can't promise the chief will agree to this, but he is a good man, with a pretty daughter much like you. I think he will be sympathetic", he smiled.

Chapter 20 — Break In

Rona was about a quarter mile from the driveway on her way back from shopping when the cell phone rang. It was Jack, wanting her to know that he had uploaded some additional documents, and the link should be waiting in her email.

For safety, she had pulled off to the side to take the call, even though she had a hands-free. As she was about to end the call, she noticed two vehicles pass her, both driving much slower than was the norm on this stretch of road.

The car in the lead was a high-end sports car, driven by a middle-aged and somewhat overweight male driver, and carrying a much younger female passenger. Rhona noted her mousy hair, pulled into a rough ponytail, and her excess makeup. Following close behind was a pickup truck, with two rather scruffy looking men in workmen's clothes.

As they neared the driveway to Roy's place, they slowed further, and then the truck turned in, while the car drove past the driveway, before pulling over to the side of the road a couple of hundred yards farther down.

"Jack, hang in there for a second. Something a bit funny is going on, and I want to take a minute to check it out." She pulled the small field glasses that she kept for occasional bird watching from under the front seat, and checking the position of the sun to ensure they would not reflect toward her quarry, put them to her eyes.

"Jack, there are two men approaching the house. Looks like one of them has a tire-iron or something similar in his hand.

"They're driving a brown two-tone truck — Ford Ranger I think. I didn't get the plate number as they passed. ..."

"No, I have no intention of going up there, but it looks like the sports car stopped just past the bend, so I am going to just 'go on my way', and see if I can catch the license as I go by. ... Yes, I'll be careful. Just stay on the line."

She slipped the car into gear and eased back off the shoulder. As she passed the driveway, the two men were screened from her vision behind the house. Rounding the slight bend, she came upon the sports car parked to the side of the road. The driver was standing outside, and appeared to have a small mobile radio in his hand.

Rhona appeared to be nonchalantly chatting on her cell as she drove by him, relaying the license plate number and other details to Jack as she did so. She continued on down the road, and then turned in at the next driveway.

Roy's neighbor ran a working farm, and Frank was in the field with a couple of his workmen when Rhona drove in. Roy had introduced her to Frank on Saturday, when they had been walking the fence line separating the two properties.

As she parked in the yard, Jack's voice popped back on the cell. "That car is registered to the supervisor at the Chemulous Plant. That isn't a social call they're making! I have his cell number, so I will call him immediately — just for a little chat! Do you have a camera?"

"There's one in my tablet. Do you want me to try to get a picture? I'm at the neighbors just down the road."

"It would be useful insurance to tie him to the location. If I can get through, the cell phone records will identify the location as well. I'd also like to know who that girl is. Just be careful they don't see you snapping pictures. These are not nice people!"

As the line went dead, Rhona heard Roy's burglar alarm go off. Good thing she had remembered to set it! Rhona again trained her field glasses on the sports car. The driver looked like he was yelling into the radio. Then she saw the girl in the car gesticulating wildly.

The girl handed him the cell phone she had taken from its holder on the dash. Even at this distance Rhona could see the man fight to compose himself, before attempting to shield the phone as the alarm siren continued to carry clearly in the still air.

"Just who he didn't want to hear from at a very inconvenient time," Rhona thought with a little smile. The conversation was brief. He leaned over to put the phone back on the dash, and then slapped his passenger hard across the face.

Rhona dumped the binoculars on the seat, and grabbed her tablet, settings it to movie mode. She was barely in time to catch the brown truck as it came barreling around the corner and stopped behind the sports car in a cloud of dust — just as the driver of the car was getting back in.

Clearly furious, he waved violently at the two men in the truck to keep moving. The truck took off again, screeching tires as it regained the pavement. Rhona thought she got a good picture as the truck roared past the end of the long driveway, followed closely by the sports car with its two occupants.

As they accelerated into the distance, Frank and his two field workers came running up to Rhona's car.

"Thought that was your car," he said. "You okay?"

"Yes, I'm fine she replied. Just glad I wasn't at home when those goons showed up."

"So am I," he replied. "You look like you could use a drink! Come on in, and we can call Roy to let him know you're all right. His alarm system is monitored, so he's probably already on his way."

"I think you're right about my needing that drink! I'll take you up on it. But I'll call Roy from here first. ... Oh no! My cell phone was in my purse, and set to 'silent ring'. Two missed calls! Roy will be frantic."

He was. Her cell call came as a great relief, but swinging into the yard only moments later, he jumped from his truck, gathered her in his arms, and just held her for a long time without speaking.

As she was about to suggest they head into the house with Frank, Rhona's cell signaled a call. "It's Jack again," she mouthed to Roy, before taking the call. Rhona was on the call only briefly.

While he thanked Frank for his kind offer, Roy was anxious to get on his way and to see what damage had been done at the house.

"Not so fast Sergeant Friday. Jack wants us to stay clear until his team arrives. Seems that they are turning up some really interesting stuff — with big implications — and if he can nail some of the low level people on easy-to-prosecute charges, he might leverage that to get to the higher ups. So we might as well take Frank up on his offer and cool our heels over a drink. ... Besides, I need to get to know my new neighbors."

Frank laughed, and looked at Roy with an amused expression that Roy translated as "Your goose is cooked." Roy shrugged, and taking Rhona's hand, headed for the house. As they climbed the steps, he saw the sheriff's car pull across the end of his driveway, lights flashing, ensuring no entrance or exit. The alarm had finally timed out, and silence settled back on the countryside.

They spent the next hour talking about farming, water issues, and the independence of young people today. Frank had always had a soft spot for Shelley, remembering her thirteen-year-old exuberance and her endless questions about the crops and soil.

He had watched her turn into a delightful and independent young woman. It was clear to him that Rhona had already become very attached to Shelley — as well as to Shelley's Dad!

As Frank was about to refresh the drinks, Jack's official-looking car pulled in — followed by a second unmarked car with two additional agents, and an unmarked panel van.

Roy met Jack at the door, and introduced him to Frank. After a few pleasantries, Jack thanked Frank for providing a spot for Roy and Rhona to hang out while they did not have access to their own property. He then asked Roy and Rhona to accompany him to the car. Four additional agents from the two other vehicles met them there.

Rhona related again precisely what she had seen. She then showed them the video she had taken. One of the technicians from the van had her rerun the part where the truck had burned back onto the pavement. "Nice of him to leave a rubber sample he laughed. So that was just there on the bend?"

Rhona nodded. "Go see what you can find," Jack said. As the technical people headed off, Jack turned to Rhona. "That video gives us much of what we need to nail this lot in court. I will need you to send a copy to me ASAP."

Jack looked back at his notes. "You mentioned that he roughed her up — probably because she answered my call, rather than letting the cell just ring. That slap could help loosen her tongue, once we split them up for interrogation."

"Why would he not have taken the call," Roy asked? "Wouldn't that look suspicious too?"

"Not really. In court, he could claim he didn't have the cell phone with him, so the fact the cell records point to this location would not have been enough to establish that he was here — not just his phone. Once she answered, and passed me over to him, he realized that argument would not fly, so he vented his frustration on her. I really want to get her into interrogation.

"It's important to establish why they paid this visit. Since Pete abruptly quit his job, and a couple of days later Chemulous was raided, it is safe to assume they suspect that he fingered them. There should not be any way they could know about Rhona's involvement. So it was probably just a fishing expedition, or possibly an attempt at intimidation."

Rhona broke in. "I hope they didn't get to my computer. I didn't back up the material I have organized so far — and if they found my notes they would know for sure that I am working on the case!"

"Well, between the Sheriff's men and my agents, we should have most of the heavy lifting done by now. Maybe it's time for us to have a look."

Roy didn't need a second invitation! When they arrived in the yard, they found one of the agents just brushing off a mold, revealing the better part of a boot impression, taken from the fine dust to the side of the path. The glass panel of the rear door had been smashed, but the Sheriff's men figured that was as far as they got. The lock was still in place, and the broken glass on the inside floor did not look disturbed.

"Okay, I think we're good to go inside. It looks like the combination of the alarm and Rhona's call to me, followed by my immediate call to them, was enough to dissuade them from going further."

...

Rhona cleaned up the broken glass, while Roy worked to pry off the molding, remove the remaining pieces of glass, and measure the opening for a new pane. Roy then headed into town with the measurements, returning shortly with a replacement pane, this one reinforced with a welded wire mesh. He busied himself putting in the replacement, while Jack wrapped up discussions with Rhona.

"I am going to provide a 24/7 surveillance team. One of the day-shift operatives will also act as liaison, so if you need additional information from us, he will be the go-to person when I'm not available. Anything else before I head out?"

At that moment the phone rang. Rhona signaled for Jack to hang on. The call display indicated 'out of area'. "Might be the kids with a progress update. I'm sure they had a better day than we did."

Even as she said it, something stirred in the pit of her stomach — an unease that seemed more than just the aftermath of the break in.

Chapter 21 — Grilling

Shelley was calling from the small office in the police station, while José and the chief talked outside. The last report that the chief received from the hospital had been cryptic and brief, saying only that Pete had lost a lot of blood, was stable, but currently still unconscious.

Shelley tried to keep herself calm as she explained what had happened, which was all the more difficult given Rhona's obvious panic on the other end of the line.

Shelley explained the events again to Roy, and asked how much she could or should tell the chief. The chief had been very sympathetic, as José had said he would be, but as a professional, wanted some answers in exchange for facilitating her trip to the coast to see Pete.

She heard a short discussion in the background, and then Jack came on the line. He asked to talk to the chief directly. Shelley went to the office door, and relayed the request.

As he took the phone, the chief motioned to Shelley that she should stay, pointing to the chair opposite his desk.

"Si Señor, I do know him ... quite well in fact. ... Yes, he is one of the best we have. If all of our Federal agents were as effective as he.... Si... Si... No, I was not aware of this, but that explains a lot of what has been going on. ... No, I do understand the protocol, but appreciate what you have been able to share.

"Yes, the plant is currently locked down by the Federales. They brought a large force, so the events at Rafael's farm did not delay them. ... Yes, of course. I have already arranged that! My daughter, Renata, will accompany José and Señorita Shelley to the coast. They will leave right away, just as soon as Renata is packed."

Si …. Yes, I will do that. I can probably arrange that at the same place. Give me a few minutes, and I will call you back to confirm. You have been very helpful, and I hope we have an opportunity to meet in person at some point. "

As he hung up the phone, he noted Shelley's surprised expression. He smiled broadly. "Yes, you are excused from the 'police grilling', and yes, you were going to Puerto Peñasco whether you cooperated or not.

"But if I send José off by himself on a road trip with such a pretty Señorita, my daughter will, I think your expression is 'have my hide'," he chuckled. "So Renata will accompany you there, and you will stay at a resort condo that is managed by a friend of mine."

"You and Renata will share a room," he added pointedly. "José has gone to pick her up, so you should be on your way in a very few minutes. You can wait for them in the outside office. I must get back on the job. Good luck to you and your injured friend, Señorita."

Shelley thanked him for his kindness and headed for the door.

"Oh yes," he added, "I almost forgot. Your FBI friend asked me to let you know that your dad and Pete's mom will be down as well, and will meet you at the hospital. I will give them the contact information for the resort, and I will see if my friend can get them accommodation as well.

"It is not so busy in this season"

Ten minutes later José poked his head in the door. "Time to go, Señorita Shelley."

Outside was another surprise. Rather than a police cruiser, idling quietly in the parking lot was a shiny yellow Chevrolet convertible of '60s vintage. In the front seat, Shelley could see a dark ponytail bobbing as the Chief's daughter leaned into the back to organize her bags.

As José opened the door, she turned from her task, raised her sunglasses, securing them on her forehead, and looked with sympathy at Shelley. She held out her hand. "I'm Renata. You must be Shelley. I am so sorry to hear of your friend's shooting. The hospital in Puerto Peñasco is very good, so I am sure he is under good care."

She slid over on the broad bench seat to make room for Shelley, and incidentally stake her claim to the driver. José eased the car onto the road, as Renata continued.

"We can be there in a couple of hours. It is beautiful on the coast, so perhaps you will be able to relax a little and enjoy the trip. I have been hoping for an opportunity for José and I to go down to the resort ever since I got back from school.

"My father is very conservative in these things, but he was also very aware that sending his future son-in-law off to a resort area with a very pretty American girl would not have been a good idea. He would not have had much peace at home!"

Her dark eyes flashed as she spoke, and Shelley felt both a kinship and a competitiveness in her manner. As they reached the main road, and the big car settled into a rhythm, José reached his arm around her. "You know I don't chase other girls," he said, giving her an affectionate squeeze.

"Maybe you don't chase them, but they chase you, and I don't see you always run away all that fast!" she retorted. She stretched up and pecked him on the cheek, then settled back and pulled her sunglasses into place from their storage perch in her thick dark hair.

They drove on in silence for some time. Shelley really liked her new acquaintances, but felt like an intruder in their space. And seeing Renata cuddled close to José only intensified her loneliness, and worry about Pete. That he was reported as still unconscious was her biggest concern.

They passed a small farm, where a few cows and some goats were grazing contentedly. José took in the scene before suddenly remembering.

"Oh, I forgot to mention, Señorita, that my father and Rafael rounded up Esmeralda and her kids, and Rafael is taking them in your friend's truck over to Rafael's new farm near Los Algodones. The keys were in the truck, and although it apparently has a few bullet holes and a missing back window, it is still drivable. My father arranged the details. I hope your friend does not mind. Rafael will get the window repaired after he has unloaded the animals."

"I am sure that Pete will be okay with that," Shelley replied.

They passed through Sonoyta, and headed southwest toward Puerto Peñasco. "We should be there in just over an hour," Renata offered.

Shelley nodded in acknowledgement. She would normally be fascinated by the desert, and naturally gregarious in the presence of other young people, but somehow her view kept turning inward and re-running that moment when she saw the gunman at the window, and saw Pete fall. Her companions, understanding her mood, talked quietly in Spanish, and did not press her to communicate.

A half hour passed and a mountain range came up on their right – clearly volcanic, and quite unlike the mountains at home. Looking up the canyons, Shelley shuddered at how circumstances had changed since that afternoon in the canyon when she had been ordered to get her "pretty butt in gear".

Now Miss-Leave-Them-Laughing-When-You-Go might be the one tragically saying goodbye, and trying to figure out how to put her life back together.

And then there was Rhona and Roy. She had been so pleased with their obvious attraction, and had looked forward to merging the two families. With Pete gone, Rhona would be a constant reminder of what might have been, as would Shelley for her. Did either of them have the strength to deal with that? And how would Roy cope if Pete's death and Shelley's involvement came between him and Rhona? Even as she ran these scenarios through her head, she marveled that this was so out of character for her. She was the one that was always "up".

She tried to focus her attention on the Pinacate Peaks, which she knew was a part of the Gran Desierto de Altar Biosphere Reserve – a 600 square mile area of volcanic peaks with tremendously varied plants, animals, reptiles and birds – exactly the kind of area that would normally fascinate her, and provide that exhilarating lift that she always felt in the desert. Today they only reminded her of Pete. Try as she might, she could not shake the feeling of dread.

The peaks soon gave way to large sand dunes and they passed a farming community to the left, and a few miles on, another to the right. "Only about another 12 kilometers to the General Hospital", José commented.

They crossed the highway that came in from the northwest, and Shelley could see the small town of Puerto Peñasco and the resorts of Rocky Point to the right on the coast.

Chapter 22 — Puerto Peñasco

A couple of miles further on, José turned abruptly to the left, and pulled to a stop in front of the hospital. He came around and opened the passenger door. "We are here Señorita. We will come with you to find out how your friend is doing."

José, Renata, and Shelley approached the reception desk, where José asked about Pete. Shelley could not catch the details, but from the few words she did pick up - "no se permiten visitantes", "inconsciente", and "policía" she realized that José was being told that Pete was still unconscious, was not allowed to have visitors, and was either under police guard or this was police orders. Renata confirmed quietly that it was the former. There was a police guard on his room!

José appeared to be arguing with the receptionist, who was an older lady, and apparently not in a mood to be challenged by young people. José held his composure, and reaching in his pocket, pulled out his identification card. Shelley again heard the word "policía", and after a moment the receptionist reluctantly picked up the telephone and placed a call, handing the phone across to José.

After a very brief conversation, José broke into a sudden smile, followed by an animated and rapid exchange. He then handed the phone back to the receptionist.

"Sounds like he knows the policeman on the other end," Renata whispered. "I think perhaps someone he trained with."

José joined them, and confirmed her suspicion. "I attended police college with Hernando. We were often partners during training exercises. He is a good man." He briefly consulted the note the receptionist had given him. "This way!"

As they headed down the hall, a burly policeman turned menacingly to face them, then broke into a big smile and grabbed José in a bear hug. They conversed in an animated way, before José turned his friend to face the two women.

"Hernando, please meet my American friend Shelley, and my fiance Renata. Señorita Shelley is a companion of your charge in the room. We have clear evidence from the cellphone records that the American, Pete, was at the scene to help my neighbor, Rafael, and it was the American's 066 call that alerted our local police and the Federales of the attack on the farm."

"Yes, we have already received that report. However, our chief thought it advisable to maintain the guard, as much for the American's protection as anything else."

Hernando removed his hat briefly, nodding to the ladies. "If you wish to visit the patient, it is okay with me, but you will need to get by the head nurse! She is in there now, and she takes her charge very seriously."

As Renata passed toward the room, Hernando whispered loudly so that José was sure to hear: "Oh, and Señorita, if you ever want some background on your fiance, just talk to me. I have lots of stories I could tell you."

Renata flashed a dark look at José. "I just might take you up on that," she replied.

José grimaced, and looked pointedly at his friend, who responded by breaking into almost-suppressed laughter.

As the trio entered the room, the nurse turned from the bed and moved quickly to intercept them. Renata immediately took charge, pumping the nurse for information, and filling her in on details of why they were here. Then she turned to Shelley.

"So she can't tell me a lot, and said we need to talk to the doctor. But as far as she can tell, he is out of danger. His blood pressure is back close to where it should be. The bleeding has stopped. The bullet glanced off the skull, but with enough force to cause a small crack in the skull and a minor concussion."

The nurse moved aside to allow them to approach Pete's bed. Shelley's eyes misted up - with a mixture of gratitude that he was alive and deep concern that he appeared so helpless. His head was heavily bandaged, and his right arm was secured to the side of the bed, with two separate intravenous drips attached. Additional plumbing emerged from under the sheet, connected to a urine bag at the side of the bed. A bundle of wires ran to a monitor that appeared to be displaying Pete's heart rate and respiration.

The nurse continued in rapid fire Spanish, then turned abruptly and left. As the door closed behind her, Renata put a hand on Shelley's shoulder.

"She says you can stay for as long as you like, but to press that call button if there is any change at all - for better or worse. And to make sure that he doesn't disconnect any of the tubes. I will send José to get something for you to eat, and then we will go and get checked in. Here is my cell phone. Call us if you need anything. José's number is here. It doesn't matter what time. Just call! We will also make sure that Hernando briefs his replacement when he finishes his shift."

They left her with a plate of tacos and a coffee, but not before Renata gave her a big and very warm hug. All trace of competitiveness had vanished with the reality of Pete's situation and Shelley's care and concern.

They had been gone only about fifteen minutes when Roy and Rhona came into the room. Shelley sat in a hard chair next to the bed, holding Pete's left hand - while each filled the other in on the day's events. Rhona was relieved to see that Pete had good color and seemed to simply be sleeping peacefully. They had talked to the doctor before coming to the room.

"He said that Pete was very lucky that the bullet just grazed him. He showed us the x-rays, and said that other than the small crack and mild concussion, there does not appear to be any serious or permanent damage. Still, he pointed out that the head and brain control everything, and they will want to keep him in for a couple of days observation once he recovers consciousness. We need to be prepared for memory loss and confusion, among other things."

Shelley nodded, rather surprised that Rhona now seemed as calm as she was.

Rhona sensed her dis-ease, and hugged her around the shoulder. "Pete's a pretty tough dude. This is not the first time he has been unconscious or hospitalized. I worried myself silly when he was young, and he fell, and he broke things, and he knocked himself out, but he has always bounced back. I think he has even more incentive to bounce back this time."

They sat in silence for a few minutes, watching the monitor track Pete's heart and respiration. Then Shelley, remembering the break in, asked the question that was puzzling her.

"Do you think Pete's shooting and the break-in at home are related? How would they know we were here?"

"I asked Jack that," Roy replied, "and he thought it unlikely. He figures the assault on the farm probably was primarily to frighten Rafael - and everyone else in town - into silence. They had no way to know that you and Pete were there. It was probably just coincidence. The break-in is a different matter. That clearly targeted us, and we don't know what they know, or how they found out we were involved at all."

The nurse breezed into the room at that point, recorded data from the monitors, checked the IV, replaced the urine bag, glared menacingly at them, and disappeared in a burst of Spanish. From her demeanor, Shelley surmised they were not pleasantries. Close on her heels, the doctor came in, nodded hello to Rhona and Roy, introduced himself to Shelley, and then began to check Pete over.

When he finished, he addressed the group. "There is no evident change at this time. He might not regain consciousness for a number of hours yet. The body tends to shut down unnecessary activities when it tries to heal. Why don't you go to your hotel? You can leave a number at reception, and we will call if there is any change."

"I would prefer to stay, if that is not against your policy," Shelley replied, once again taking hold of Pete's hand.

"I can authorize one of you staying overnight, but for you two, it would be best to get some rest," he told the parents. "You might need to stand in when the Señorita gets tired."

After the doctor left, Shelley gave her borrowed cell number to Rhonda and Roy. Since they would be checking in at the same resort, they agreed to stop in to meet José and Renata, and let them know that Shelley would be spending the night at the hospital.

"I doubt that Renata will mind that we don't share a room tonight," Shelley thought to herself.

With Roy and Rhona gone to check in, she tried to settle in for what would be a long night. She got up periodically to stretch her sore muscles. The hard wooden chair was taking a toll on her derriere.

The head nurse breezed in regularly up until about ten o'clock. On her last visit she brought a younger nurse, who was apparently taking the night shift. She then left with her usual abruptness, but returned only moments later with two pillows and a blanket, which she handed unceremoniously to Shelley. She then spun on her heels and disappeared out the door, as Shelley mumbled a surprised "mucho gracias" to her retreating back.

As the night wore on, she found it difficult to stay awake. She tried various ways to get comfortable, finally putting both pillows on the chair. By putting Pete's left arm on his pillow, and with the added height provided by the pillows under her bum, she was able to rest her head on his chest. The sound of his strong heartbeat and steady breathing was reassuring, and she soon drifted into a light sleep.

She awoke suddenly, aware of a hand exploring under her tee shirt and the strap of her sports bra along her shoulder blades. She had no idea of the time, or how long she had slept. She hardly dared to move. A quiet voice spoke in the dark. "Hmmm. No wings, and I don't think angels in heaven wear sports bra's, so this has to be my earth angel come to call me back from the abyss."

R.A. Abell

Chapter 23 — Back from the Abyss

Rhona awoke from a troubled sleep to find the message light of her cell phone flashing on the bedside table. As she rolled over and reached for the phone, Roy spoke in the dark.

"What is it? Is there news from the hospital."

Rhona, who had been unconsciously holding her breath, exhaled loudly. "Yes. It's a text message from Shelley. Pete is conscious, and the doctor is with him now. Shelley says that Pete seems 'pretty alert', and followed that with a smiley face! She says that Pete is pretty foggy about what happened, although he said he had some notion of being in a helicopter at one point.

"He is not overly impressed with being 'trussed up' and being punched full of intravenous tubes, but she figures he'll get over it. She says the doctor wants to monitor him closely for the next while, but by sometime shortly after breakfast we can probably visit."

"That's news worth waking up for", he replied, giving her hand a squeeze. "Maybe we'll both be a spot less restless for what's left of the night."

Rhona texted a short reply to Shelley, and then rolled back to cuddle up to Roy. "Yes, I'd go for that! Sleep tight."
...

They met José and Renata on the way into the hospital.

"Good morning Señor, Señora. I assume you had the good news from Señorita Shelley?"

"We did, José", Rhona replied, giving Renata a hug. "We so appreciate your interest and support."

"Well I am glad we were able to assist, Señora. By the way, the official clearance has come through, and Pete is no longer under any suspicion at all, so he will be free to go as soon as he is released from hospital.

"But he would do well to rest for a spot, so if he and señorita Shelley wish to stay with us for the rest of the week, we can make room for them, and would be pleased to have time to get to know them better. I talked with Rafael, and he has Pete's truck patched up. Renata and I can drive them to Los Algodones, and they can pick up the truck there."

"I'm sure they would like that, and I can spare them for a few days, although Rhona and I will need to get back as soon as practical," Roy responded, noting Renata's raised eyebrows and coy smile when José mentioned '...making room for them.' He very much liked this young couple, and sensed that for Pete and Shelley this might well be a lasting friendship. "Before we go, though, I think Rhona is hoping for a trip to Bird Island."

"Well, if you are here for a couple more days, perhaps we can all go. Renata checked the boat schedule before we left the condo today, and there is a boat going in two days. I believe that the señorita is an ecologist, so she would surely enjoy a trip there. Hopefully Pete will be released by then as well."

As they entered the room, they found Pete sitting up in bed, his arm draped over Shelley's shoulder, as the nurse snapped a picture on Shelley's camera. Shelley insisted they all pose again, then thanked the nurse quietly as the others greeted Pete.

"By the way," she asked, "the nurse who was on yesterday seemed so gruff, yet she brought me blankets and stuff. That surprised me!"

"Well señorita, as a nurse myself, I know that it can be difficult to have a patient whom you think you might lose. We can get attached, and I think the Head nurse has been in the business for many years. She is really a kind person, and I think that 'gruffness' as you call it, is a bit of defense to not care too much. One finds it often with older nurses."

"Yes, that makes sense when you put it that way. Thank you."
...

Two days later, Pete was on the boat with everyone else. He still had a bandage on his head, and strict orders to stay out of the water – and away from the Margaritas - but he was there! The day was very clear and calm. Shelley was fascinated with the number and variety of birds, the casual poses of the sea lions lounging on the rocks, and the constant feeding frenzy, as the pelicans and boobies dive-bombed the schools of fish near the rocky point between the small islands. But most of the time, she stayed cuddled close to Pete.

When they returned from the excursion, Roy and Rhona said their goodbyes to the young people, and headed for home, a five or six hour trip, putting them in late in the evening. The four new friends ate at a small but busy seafood restaurant in the Malecon, overlooking the harbor. Then, as the seemingly endless line of pelicans headed southwest into the setting sun, they made their way back to the condo.

As they left the car, Renata pulled Shelley aside. "About 'our' room, I am trusting that my conservative Catholic father will not have another opportunity to 'interrogate' you – at least not until after José and I are married, and José is promoted. Or would you prefer that I be your roommate while you are here?"

Shelley noted the trademark raised eyebrow, then pulled Renata into a hug. "Deal, no interrogation. But I hope that warrants an invite to the wedding!"

...

When they parted four days later, it was hugs all round. Rafael's wife had insisted they all stay for dinner, so it was early evening when they said adios to Rafael and his family, to Renata and José, and with Shelley at the wheel of Pete's old truck, headed for the border.

"It will be good to be home," Pete commented.

"Yes, for sure. But is not going to feel quite as secure after the break in."

Chapter 24 — Connections

Jack came out to the house the following day to say hello, and see if Shelley and Pete might have any insights into the break in. As Rhona reran the video yet again, Pete became agitated.

"Okay. So they **were** after me! Shelley, you recognize this girl?"

"She sure looks familiar! Isn't she one of the 'professionals' from that flophouse you were staying in? The one that was asking all the questions about your quitting your job? I could have been suspicious that she seemed so interested in you. Looks like she was on your former boss's payroll — maybe for more than one service!"

"Yes," Pete replied. "Oh, and before I forget, hold on a second...."

He disappeared into the bedroom, returning with two small paper documents stapled on one corner. "My prof has copies, but this one is his report on what he found on Shelley's filter. He signed it, and this is his contract information. The other is his critique of the supposed 'research' paper suggesting use of these same chemicals for weather modification."

Jack flipped through the documents briefly. "This provides a whole other dimension to the investigation," he said. "Can you also send me soft copy? My public email is on my card. Don't include the files, just drop me a note. I'll get back to you with a link for secure file transfer."

He looked again at the first report before adding: "Rhona, you might want to send a copy of both documents to the Senator. The agriculture folks in Arizona will be very interested to know what might be ending up in their produce. I am sure the Senator will know how to turn up the heat there to help counter pressure from the Armed Services Committee representative."

Rhona spent Tuesday morning in the company books, and on the phone to her Senator and Congressmen. All three had good reason to ask questions in places where she could not, and once these questions were out there in the political sphere, they tended to take on a life of their own.

The Senator understood the protocol, and rather than pressing her on details of links to the Armed Services Committee, had agreed to call Jack to discuss this later that morning. That would also allow him to discuss the Mexican connection. He attached considerable importance to making the investigation "international" immediately. That would give him a reason to raise it directly with the President when they met on Thursday.

He summed up his position when he told Rhona: "In my experience, when I'm told something has to be withheld from the public for 'security' reasons, in ninety-nine cases out of one hundred, it is the security of someone's massive profits that is really behind all the secrecy. Either that, or a case of boys playing with expensive toys — with either no clue about or no concern for the potentially destructive consequences of their play."

Jack called just after two. He had filled the Senator in on the family connections and stock holdings of his colleague, and also let him know that the FBI and Federal agents in Mexico had a joint operation planned to simultaneously seize vehicles on each side of the border carrying waste into Mexico from the plant near Pecos. Since the trucks typically traveled in convoys of two to four vehicles, it would be an easy matter to split them up at the border. They had a convoy of three under surveillance that would hit the border in the next half hour. Two would make it across and run into the Mexican officers a mile down the road.

"Did you get anything out of your interrogation?" She asked. "I'm assuming your team made the arrests last night?

"Yes," Jack replied. "The female in custody was quite forthcoming. He had roughed her up pretty good, but in her line of business that is not uncommon. She is not the sharpest tack in the box, and she really seemed to think they didn't want to do more than talk to Pete. She figured out they intended more than that only after the alarm went off."

"One might wonder if she could be that naive, but statements from the two thugs we picked up in the truck seems to corroborate it, so we will provide protective custody, and use her testimony to put Pete's supervisor away for a long time."

"When we interrogated him, he was pretty cocky — and so was his lawyer — until we showed them the video, and he found out we had his two thugs in custody as well. They went a bit green when we asked questions about the Pecos and Mexican operations, the lawyer in particular — which I found interesting."

"I'll send you information on his firm. Among those 'deleted' emails we recovered, along with the payables, you might want to keep an eye out for his law firm. My guess is that they are up to their neck in this, and well aware they are operating outside the law. By the time we finished, the lawyer was sweating profusely and clearly more concerned about himself than about his client."

"I'll watch for that email," Rhona replied. "Something to keep Roy occupied for a few hours. I'm expecting them home pretty early. Pete and Shelley are anxious to find out more about that geoengineering 'researcher' who published the articles on weather modification. There has to be a connection, since he recommended almost the exact mix of chemicals that Chemulous produced."

...

Pete and Shelley showed up just after four. "Roy will be along shortly," Shelley said. "He went to the Chinese restaurant to get some takeout food."

"Yes, he just called to make sure I didn't have something already on," Rhona replied. "Given the time lines we are on, I told him that was a good call. ... So you are going to check out that university 'research' now?"

"Already started!" Pete said. "We had a spot of time over lunch, and we found a full list of all grants by department and project. It lists dates, amounts, and donors for each grant. I downloaded the list, so I'll go upload it to the server, and we can start doing some cross checking. The name of the Grants officer is there as well, along with a rather self-aggrandizing write-up touting his success in bringing in money."

"No doubt it directly affects his compensation, so he would not be too fussy about where it came from," she replied. "Research dollars, and the success of the football team, seem to be the most important metrics for many university administrators these days. There was a time when they actually focused on academic excellence and independent scientific research, as strange as that might sound today."

It didn't take Rhona long to find what she was looking for. Over three years, there were three separate quarter-million-dollar grants to the university for geoengineering research by a company called JMX-Research Services. The company had no Web presence, but was registered in Delaware."

"Yes! ... Registered by the same legal firm that Jack had referenced in their conversation earlier in the day. Their registered office addresses were the same. Just as Roy walked in with the Chinese food, she found the payables to JMX in the books. Monthly, and adding up to nearly four hundred thousand a year! *"Another one hundred fifty thousand to spread around. Wonder who else is on the payola list,"* she thought.

...

They took time to enjoy the fast food, but couldn't resist shoptalk, comparing notes and planning their next line of inquiry.

After supper they all settled in, Rhona taking on the company books, while Roy scanned the hundreds of recovered emails for companies, organizations, and individuals that might link the pieces together.

Shelley was gathering all of the evidence and data indicating widespread increases in the specific chemicals — in everything from water to increased levels of arsenic in crops like rice.

Meanwhile, Pete continued his investigation of the funded university research. By ten o'clock, Pete's database on the server had grown substantially. Shelley added information showing that water contamination patterns with the expected profile were widespread in the surrounding states, particularly in a large area of California north of L.A. Pete found the "researcher" named in a number of postings, including submissions to geoengineering conferences, and some on open forums where former students had some not very complimentary things to say about the research, one calling the whole geoengineering department "bogus".

Roy's email searches turned up the most interesting find! Someone who appeared to be a senior officer in the air force, but using a personal email, had contacted Chemulous saying that questions were being raised about the program "... in some quarters...." He suggesting his compensation was low for the risks involved, and he might have to "spread some money around to keep the lid on". Roy found a terse reply: "Joe has okayed an extra 100k. Expect it by the usual channel, four instalments."

"That probably accounts for two thirds of the extra payments to JMX Research," Rhona said. "I also wonder who 'Joe' is, but that will have to wait until tomorrow. My neck is getting stiff from too many hours at this computer. So I am shutting down for tonight."

"I could give your neck and shoulders a massage," Roy replied brightly.

"I've discovered in the comparatively short time I've known you that your massages have a tendency to start out quite innocently, but then quickly turn into something else," she mused, as her computer screen went black.

"Is that a bad thing?"

"No, just an observation. I didn't say it was bad," she laughed. "So why is your computer still running?"

Chapter 25 — Lights Out

Wednesday morning, as all four were sitting down to breakfast, Rhona took a call from Jack.

"Rhona, tell your team that things are speeding up! Better yet, can you put me on speaker phone?"

She clicked the speaker phone button, and Jack continued.

"The task force working with the Mexican authorities intercepted the waste shipment yesterday, and took the drivers into custody. We have the fake manifests, and photo evidence that at least one driver stopped and switched the dangerous-goods labeling while on the road.

"The Mexican police caught a border guard pocketing an envelope of bills that came from the driver of the lead truck, and that driver is now in custody in Mexico. Because he is an American Citizen, that arrest is already triggering intergovernmental discussions on the diplomatic front.

"We also have lab results that our experts say clearly tie the military cleanup site in New Mexico, the contents of those trucks, and the Mexican disposal and processing site in Rafael's home town. The Mexican government has sent health and environmental assessment teams into the facility, and taken two more local government people in for questioning.

"With the link to the cross-border transportation of dangerous goods, that is going to stir the pot up here north of the border as well."

"So what I need from you is a quick preliminary report that allows us to show how wide this goes, clearly establishes this as 'a conspiracy, and gives us additional grounds for search and seizure."

"I have a meeting scheduled bright and early tomorrow morning with the Department of Justice in Washington. About the same time, the Senator is meeting with the President, and has arranged to have a couple of Congressmen representing agricultural districts in California and Arizona with him," Jack continued.

"My flight leaves Phoenix at five-twenty, and I want to put my case together on the way to Washington, and discuss the more 'public' pieces with the Senator at the hotel tonight. Can you get me something by four? I know that doesn't give you much time."

When Jack hung up, Roy looked perplexed.

"Damn. We really need to be here to help, but Pete and I have a meeting with the power company today. Pete is pitching his proposal to use the power line right-of-way to mount solar arrays, creating a joint venture that is a triple win, for them, for us, and for the environment. It's his idea, so I want him out front — but as the CEO with signing authority, I need to be there as well."

"At this point, I think we have enough information for Jack's purposes, so Shelley and I can probably get the report together, as long as there are no technical issues," Rhona replied.

"I'm glad to see 'your' daughter is not distracting Pete so much he ceases to be useful," she added with a grin — and a wink at Shelley.

"More inspiration than distraction," Pete volunteered.

"Let's go with that!" Shelley laughed. ... "What time will you be back?"

Roy looked at his watch. "We can probably make it by two. We can take two vehicles, in case we don't both need to be there the whole time."

Shelley handed her car keys to Pete. "For such an important quest, Lancelot had best have a fresh horse to impress the foreign potentates."

...

By one-thirty Rhona and Shelley had all of the information organized, and were working on the final formatting. Rhona wanted the report uploaded to Jack's secure server no later than three-thirty. It would be a close thing.

Suddenly her screen went black, and the house went totally quiet. Shelley came into the office just as Rhona was grabbing her cell phone to call Roy.

"We got out of the meeting a while ago, and I am almost home. I'll be there in two minutes," he replied after hearing what had happened. "Do you know if the power is out at Frank's as well? ... Wait a second! There's a panel van parked by the utility pole at our fence line. Strange though, it doesn't look like the usual utility company truck. I'll stop and see what's up."

"Is Pete with you?" Rhona asked anxiously.

"He had to stop for gas. He should be here momentarily. There are a couple of guys just putting a ladder back on top of the van. I'm just getting out to talk to them."

Rhona was about to tell him to be careful when she heard a muffled couple of words, and then the line went dead.

"I have a bad feeling about this," Rhona said to Shelley. "See if you can get Pete on his cell. I'm going to alert Bill. Because of the curve in the road, the agents will not be able see the far fence line from Frank's side."

Shelley went back into her room to grab her cell phone with Pete's cell number. From her window she could see the unmarked van about 100 yards away — and the two men, who appeared to be arguing with her father. Suddenly one of them stepped behind Roy, pinning his arms from the back, while the other opened the rear door of the van!

Chapter 26 — Reflex

Pete came round the corner, and took in the scene in an instant. Clearly these men were trying to force Roy into the van. At that moment, Pete heard his cell phone ring.

"The call will have to wait," he thought, as he pulled to a stop and jumped out of the car. Roy saw him out of the corner of his eye, and as the man pinning his arms rotated toward this new threat, Roy used his weight to push the man back, pinning him between Roy and the door of the van.

The second man grabbed a wrench from the truck, and advanced toward Pete. "This is a private matter friend, so just get back in that little car and get the hell out of here!" he threatened, holding the wrench out in front.

Pete said nothing, but stood his ground. The thug was probably four to six inches taller, and outweighed him by a good forty pounds.

Roy yelled "Look out!" as the thug suddenly took three quick steps toward Pete, raising the wrench above his head. Roy watched in what seemed like slow motion as the man lunged forward, only to suddenly rise off his feet, fly over top of Pete — who was in a partial crouch — and land very heavily on his back on the pavement a good six feet further down the road.

At that moment, Bill appeared around the left side of the van, gun already drawn.

...

From the window, Shelley saw the Sheriff's car pull up, and saw the FBI agents hustle one prisoner into the car, hands cuffed in front of him. The second thug took a little longer, as he was clearly in major pain, but they finally got him in as well. The Sheriff went back and retrieved the wrench, carefully placing it in a clear plastic bag and sealing the end.

She watched as Roy and Pete removed the ladder from the truck and propped it against the utility pole. Pete climbed a few feet up, and suddenly she heard the computers beep, and the normal house sounds return.

Rhona came into Shelley's room, and surveyed the scene on the road below. "Thank God they're both okay," she said. Shelley just threw her arms around Rhona's neck, and Rhona felt the shudder that went through Shelley's whole body. They just clung to each other for several minutes, not speaking. Finally, Rhona eased her grip and looked at Shelley.

"They are both really important to each of us. But that's all the more reason we have to get this report finished. I had just saved my version when the power died, so I doubt that I lost much of anything. How about you?"

"I'm not sure exactly when I saved last, but my machine has rebooted and is back up, so I'll see if the document auto-recovers before going to a backup," Shelley replied. "We lost a good hour to the blackout, so that gives us only another hour to get this formatted and uploaded."

Rhona was on her way back to the office when Roy and Pete came in. After hugs all round, Roy put his arm around Pete's shoulder. "It has been a 'challenging' day to put it mildly. I need a drink — or two. Could I interest anyone in a beer?"

"You two go ahead — and get some steak out for the barbecue while you are at it. Shelley and I still have some work ahead to get this report off to Jack."

They missed their self-imposed deadline by five minutes, but Rhona got a call from Jack at a quarter to four saying that he had the report, had taken a quick look at it, and was certain that it would be enough to get the investigation sanctioned by the DOJ.

"Oh yes," he added, "Bill just sent me a list of phone numbers from the cell phone in that van. Seems there was an entry for 'Joe'. Just maybe the 'Joe' mentioned in your report. The number traces to an officer barracks at an airbase in the state. I am pretty sure we will get permission to track the calls from that number."

"I have to get moving now, or I will miss my Washington flight. I'll try to get back to you tomorrow on the outcome of the meeting, unless I am told to keep everything strictly internal — which could happen."

After they were off the call, Rhona and Shelley gave each other a big hug, and went to join the guys on the deck. "So where are our drinks?" Rhona asked.

Pete put down his beer. "My Mom is a frozen-Margarita fan, especially with prickly pear, but it's the wrong season for cactus fruit, so it will have to be plain. Will that suit my beautiful Señorita?" he asked Shelley, getting to his feet.

Shelley kissed him. "Consider that my answer — to a whole lot of questions!" she replied. "And speaking of questions, what's with the heroics out there on the road? That guy with the wrench was substantially bigger than you. I had a panic attack. This is the second time I've thought I was going to be a widow before I was a wife. I think I actually yelled 'run' at the top of my voice. Like you could hear me from here!"

Pete looked mildly embarrassed.

"Let me answer that, while Pete makes those drinks," Rhona interjected. "First things first! And yes you did yell. I was on the cell with Bill, and he heard you clearly — even though you were in the other room! He thought **we** were being attacked," she laughed.

She waived Pete towards the kitchen, before continuing. "If you hadn't mistaken me for some floozy, and had been in Pete's place in Tucson, you might already know this. More or less at my insistence, I think he has at least one small trophy on display there."

"He spent all four years of his undergrad on the Judo team. Being Pete, he was never into bragging about it, in spite of winning several championships, always against bigger opponents. So in a situation like today, it was pretty much instinct — or at least habit."

"I thought he was crazy to even get out of the car," Roy mused, "and totally cracked to stand there while that thug came at him with that big wrench. Pete looked so calm that I thought he had lost it. And of course that just made that punk madder!"

"And speaking of crazy to even get out of the car," Rhona replied sharply, "whatever were **you** thinking?"

"I guess I wasn't," Roy replied sheepishly. "I'm not as used to this 'cloak and dagger' stuff as you are. My mind was on the meeting we had just finished, and it never occurred to me that those guys might be up to no good. Sorry to have given you a scare."

"Well, as 'w' words go, like Shelley, I prefer 'wife' to 'widow'," she replied nonchalantly. "Anyway, I'm glad nothing more serious happened. So your apology is accepted. Just realize that Jack did not assign two agents 24/7 just to humor me. Now I better get some salad happening, and the barbecue should be started, and then we need some wine."

As she headed into the house, Roy looked at Shelley. "That's twice in five minutes that the 'wife' word has come up. Have I missed something?"

"Oh probably," Shelley laughed. "But then guys can be dense at times. Anyway, I am going to go get a bottle of wine, while you fire up the gas. Then, both Rhona and I want to know how your meetings went today."

Pete arrived with the Margarita just as Shelley was opening the wine to let it breathe. Roy had turned on the gas barbecue, and was sitting staring into his beer glass when Rhona returned with the salad, and a container of vegetables to go on the barbecue.

Roy watched her graceful and self-assured movements as she busied herself putting the vegetables on, and setting out the plates. It was as if she belonged here; as if she had always belonged here.

He thought back to the early days with Jane and wondered — for perhaps the four-hundredth time — where that relationship had gone wrong. Or perhaps started wrong! Rhona interrupted his self-commiseration.

"Okay. So those vegetables will take about ten minutes longer than the steak. Is that enough time for you to fill us in on how the meeting went with the utility company?"

"Should be," Roy replied. "It's not a complicated story. But Pete did a great job describing the technical side from our perspective. They had a couple of typical hard-nosed engineers there who started to raise a bunch of objections, but he diffused that pretty effectively."

"How did you do that?" Shelley asked Pete. "I would think they would know a lot more — especially on the electrical side — than you do, clever as you are."

"Yeah, that's what I told them," Pete laughed. "I let them get all of the issues on the floor, and then I said that the technical electrical stuff was not my bag, but that I had every confidence that once they understood the economics they would be clever enough to find solutions to all the very-real problems. Then I threw the ball to Roy. He had the numbers to back that up."

"Once the executives had a handle on the economics, they pretty well repeated what Pete had said," Roy added. "They said they would put a team of engineers on it, and were confident that any issues could be resolved. So we got to the point of a memorandum of agreement, including a phase one study and pilot to happen before the end of the year."

"Congratulations," Rhona said. "I gather this project will have a big upside for RoySolar?"

"Well, we're not out of the woods yet," Roy replied, "but if we can get all of the approvals, and the Utility Company backs the financing, which they seem committed to do, it will generate a steady income stream for the foreseeable future. We will be crazy busy over the summer.... But speaking of busy, I need to get busy with those steaks."

"Yes you do, and then we can start on the salad. I don't know about anyone else, but I'm starving. ... Not much wonder, looking at the time. In another hour, Jack will be in Washington."

Chapter 27 — Buy-in

It was barely past eight in the morning when Jack called. On Eastern Time, he was already out of his meeting.

"We've got the green light from DOJ. It is full steam ahead with the investigation! The Attorney General was very impressed with what your team was able to piece together in such a short time," he told Rhona. "It is going to take probably six months to get the full case put together, so you will be pretty busy for a while, but it probably will also be good for your retirement fund!"

"The Senator apparently had a good meeting with the President and his assistants. He suggests you might want to tune in to the Presidential address that is already scheduled for Tuesday evening."

"He thinks there is going to be a 'weather change', if you'll excuse the pun. And apparently a couple of the Senator's colleagues have decided to stand down from the Armed Services Committee and, in fact, will be retiring from politics at the end of their term. That could mean burying some things that should be public, but it's a trade-off to get the rest of this out in the open without political interference."

"Washington hasn't changed much, has it," Rhona replied.

"I'm wouldn't hold my breath for that," Jack replied, "but we should at least put a big dent in this particular operation."

...

The President was probably about two thirds of the way through his address to the nation when he raised the topic.

"It has come to the attention of my office in the last week that some information that we have from certain quarters — specifically regarding experiments related to climate change being carried out in the atmosphere over the U.S. mainland — might have been deliberately misleading."

"At the same time, there have been suggestions from some groups that technological methods could safely reduce the rate of global warming without negative effects. These have been challenged by others, amid concerns that large-scale experiments are already taking place. The implicated departments have consistently denied such experiments are being conducted."

"As a consequence of very recent work by the FBI, and with the support of the Department of Justice, we now have substantial evidence of collusion and conspiracy on the part of individuals and groups who have both distorted the research, and also acted in a manner that could be considered dangerous to the health and well being of the general population."

"I have therefore signed, as of this morning, an executive order to immediately halt any and all of these activities until a full review of the extent and the safety of these experiments is determined."

"To that end, I will be convening an advisory committee on the topic normally referred to as 'geoengineering'. This committee will be broadly based, and will include ecologists, agricultural experts, public health experts, biologists, botanists, chemists, and climate scientists, including giving an equal voice to those who have previously raised serious concerns of long-term effects."

"This committee will advise my office on the safety and possible negative consequences of both research into, and long-range application of such technologies. Serious questions have been raised, and it is important for our country and for the entire World to avoid potentially irreversible actions without the broadest possible consensus on the advisable courses of action."

"As for the apparent conspiracy, the white house will be supporting both the DOJ and the call by the Senator from California for a full Senate inquiry into how this might have been facilitated, and what departments were knowingly or unknowingly complicit in these actions."

"While some persons are already in custody, we expect a number of additional individuals will be investigated, and additional arrests are anticipated."

...

"Wow! Who would have imagined that chasing towhees in a canyon in Arizona would end up triggering a speech from the President," Shelley exclaimed.

"It should not be difficult to rally the solar community or the agricultural community behind the President's initiative," Roy commented. "Every one will be in agreement on clear skies and clean water."

"That's true, Rhona replied, but expect a huge reaction from right-wing think tanks. The disinformation mill will go into high gear. The fossil fuel industry wants the climate data inconsistent, and as a group would prefer to push a technology solution to global warming at the very same time they claim that it is just 'a normal geological cycle'.

"If the solutions proposed use huge amounts of fossil fuel, so much the better."

"The involvement of the military in this affair means that some people high up view climate control as a potential weapon, and they want to pursue this regardless of the dangers, or international agreements," she continued.

"And the military doesn't have a habit of paying attention to the possible long-term costs to everyone else. You only need look at nuclear weapons research, biological and chemical weapons research, actual chemical use like Agent Orange, and over two hundred thousand veterans suffering from Gulf War Syndrome to realize that. So we are a long way from out of the woods yet."

"Jack's estimate of at least six months to build the case is probably low. I sure hope the big push is over before Christmas. With your utility project, and the kids' studies, we are all going to need a good break by then. ... But right now, something to drink seems in order before we turn in for the night."
...

An hour later, Roy was staring at the ceiling. As he adjusted his pillow for the fourth or fifth time, Rhona took his hand.

"You're very restless tonight," she said. "Something on your mind?"

"Well yeah, I seem to be rolling a lot of stuff around. It has been something of a life altering couple of weeks. Sorry if I am keeping you awake."

"That's okay," she replied. "In spite of all the commotion, I have been sleeping better here than I have for several years. I feel very at peace with myself, and very happy things have turned out as they have. So if you want to talk, let's talk."

"I guess that is one of the things that I really need to get used to," he replied, rolling to face her in the dim light of the projector clock on the ceiling, " — the fact that we can talk, and do talk about a whole range of things. That has made me realize that with Jane, I never had that experience. She was always so bound up in what she was doing and thinking, that my issues — and Shelley's issues — always seemed to take a back seat."

"I guess the good thing was that Shelley and I built a bond that has lasted. When I see Shelley and Pete together, and the easy banter and camaraderie they have, it makes me especially happy for them. I like Pete a lot. He seems to have all of the best qualities I could ask for in a possible son-in-law, and the fact that he is proving so adept in the business is a bonus."

"But I am still old fashioned enough to be conscious much of the time that Pete is in that other room sleeping with my little girl! My twenty-five old little girl," he laughed.

"At the same time, having had Jane announce that she was sleeping with her French instructor, and having her throw her wedding ring in my face, did shake me up in ways that I am not sure I have fully recovered from yet."

"She really did that?" Rhona replied incredulously, giving his hand an extra squeeze.

"Yes, and walked out without even saying goodbye to Shelley. We never talked to her again — just to her lawyer."

"It's very difficult for me to imagine how a person could ever behave that way," Rhona replied. "As hard as it was to lose my husband suddenly, with no warning, at least I had the consolation that he had always been there for me and for Pete, and probably still is. And if he is looking in on me now, I know he would be very happy for me that I found you."

"As for my goofy and lovable son, you surely understand his intentions. Those two are so 'meant for each other' it mists me up anytime I think about them. Pete and I had a little chat about it yesterday. He seemed to think that getting married before finishing school would be a substantial expense, and he really wants to do it right."

"I pointed out that our current contract with the FBI is a whole second income, and that putting marriage off because of money is rather stupid. So between you and me, he is going 'ring' shopping tomorrow. Shelley doesn't know, so please don't say anything."

"Naturally I am very happy to hear that. Do you know what he has in mind for timing?"

"Well, as I mentioned earlier, it would be good if we could all get a break by Christmas. The bulk of my work should be finished, and it sounds like your solar project should be well advanced and into testing, so you can probably squeeze out a week or so. Pete was thinking it might be cool to take a cruise, and get married on board.

"There's a tall-ship cruise out of Los Angeles around that time that could be fun," she continued. "Would you be up for that?"

"A wedding on board a cruise ship? With a honeymoon to follow? Sounds good to me. So you'll have to find out if they have discounts for two."

Rhona smiled in the darkened room. "Are you referring to two fares, or two weddings?" she asked innocently.

"I can do this," Roy said, half to himself. "I was actually thinking — two weddings."

"As I am sure you already figured out, the answer is 'yes'. Yes to both, actually. I already asked, just in case it might be useful information. They can cut the cost by 40% over two separate weddings."

"Hard to resist a bargain, and saving money is good too, so ..."

The rest of his sentence was smothered, not that he was complaining. There is more than one way to communicate.

Author Notes for Trails

While fiction, this book deals with concepts that have been proposed by supposedly intelligent people who seem to believe that geoengineering the climate is a solution to our other destructive practices and can be carried out safely. In fact, JFK, speaking at the U.N. General Assembly in 1961 spoke enthusiastically about developing the capability for weather control.

At the same time, many have raised serious concerns that the effects could be dangerous and irreversible, and that substances used for geoengineering are toxic to both plants and animals. It is all too easy to focus on one element of a very complex system and to either deliberately ignore or be totally unaware of potential for harm in other parts of that system.

Most notable among those sounding an alarm are Rosalind Peterson who among other things has posted a You Tube video called "The Chemtrail Cover-Up". In that video, she reports on long-term studies of changes in California groundwater and issues with crops which she believes is caused by spraying of chemicals into the air.

Goggle "chemtrails" or "what are they spraying" and you will turn up dozens of claims and counterclaims, and everything from obvious stupidity to global conspiracy theory.

Understanding the scientific issues is very complex. For example, aluminum in the soil as an ingredient of common rocks and so-called "bio-available" aluminum are very different beasts. This provides an opportunity for misinformation to be disseminated — either pro or con.

That bio-available aluminum is toxic to all forms of life is very well understood among biological and medical researchers, which you can quickly confirm with a simple Goggle search.

After completing the book, I came across an article on the climate-change controversy, describing in detail how an otherwise obscure professor published an article in a "B" grade journal debunking CO_2 as a major cause of global warming.

As described, the incident was pretty much dead on with Rhona's description of the "researcher" in this novel. This low quality research has already been seized on by the fossil fuel industry for frequent reference in "debunking" articles and on "debunking" websites.

That the military considers weather control to be a military asset has been documented. That politicians and their families have worked against the best interests of citizens for party or personal benefit has also been well documented. Some specific instances of the later have been described in my non-fiction book called Salvaging Capitalism / Saving Democracy.

That people with psychopathic tendencies can rise to positions of corporate control is also well documented.

Recent research in the U.S. — on an admittedly small and not totally random sample — found that the incidence of psychopathy in some management groups is four times as high as the incidence in the general population, and that tendencies toward psychopathy can be a predictor of 'success' in rising to the top in today's mega business world.

So to imagine a company that would behave as Chemulous and its affiliates behave in this novel is regrettably all too easy. And that secrecy is key to covering up both private sector and government malfeasance is well understood and all too frequently practiced.

Pollution of air and water, and introduction of man-made species of food crops (GMOs) is highly correlated with a whole range of new diseases or "syndromes" that are then "treated" with expensive pharmaceuticals. As citizens we have a right to know what is going into our air, our water, and our food, and if we fail to insist on transparency, we will lose both our freedom and our currently still-hospitable planet.

Many politicians today seem to be "bought and paid for", and much important legislation is written by corporate lawyers and rubber stamped by the elected officials whom we carelessly assume are watching out for our interests.

So when agencies such as the FBI unit described here, or politicians like Rhona's "Senator" step up to the plate to protect our interests, we all have to be part of their support structure.

For a comprehensive look at many of the issues that appear to be currently "swept under the carpet" you can refer to http://www.agriculturedefensecoalition.org/ for some indicators. It provides insights into many different agricultural and environmental issues, from bee-colony-collapse disorder to geoengineering. It has multiple references and links to news and reports.

By our individual actions or inactions, we help build the future. Because we live in a complex world with limited visibility of the big picture, and with information often limited to someone else's version of "need to know", we can all too easily be asleep at the switch.

RA — January, 2014

About the Author

Dr. Bob Abell is a business owner, a teacher, and an environmentalist. With a Ph.D. in science education, he has a keen interest in the history of science, in ethical science, in health, business, politics, and government.

He is the author of a non-fiction published in 2012 called <u>Salvaging Capitalism — Saving Democracy</u>, and a short novel set in 2039 called <u>The Corporation</u>.

Made in the USA
Charleston, SC
28 May 2015